FORT WORTH PUBLIC LIBRARY

P9-CEJ-067

BOB HONEY
SINGS JIMMY CRACK CORN

BOB HONEY

SINGS JIMMY CRACK CORN

A NOVEL

SEAN PENN

AUTHOR OF *BOB HONEY WHO JUST DO STUFF*

RARE BIRD
LOS ANGELES, CALIF.

THIS IS A GENUINE RARE BIRD BOOK

Rare Bird Books
453 South Spring Street, Suite 302
Los Angeles, CA 90013
rarebirdbooks.com

Copyright © 2019 by Sean Penn

FIRST HARDCOVER EDITION

All rights reserved, including the right to reproduce this book
or portions thereof in any form whatsoever, including but not limited
to print, audio, and electronic.

For more information, address:
Rare Bird Books Subsidiary Rights Department
453 South Spring Street, Suite 302
Los Angeles, CA 90013

Set in Warnock
Printed in the United States

Cover Design by Gabrielle Yakobson
Interior Design by Hailie Johnson

10 9 8 7 6 5 4 3 2 1

Library of Congress Cataloging-in-Publication Data

Names: Penn, Sean, 1960– author.
Title: Bob Honey Sings Jimmy Crack Corn: A Novel / by Sean Penn.
Description: Los Angeles, CA : Rare Bird Books, [2019]
Identifiers: LCCN 2019019667 | ISBN 9781644280584 (alk. paper)
Subjects: | GSAFD: Black humor (Literature) | Satire.
Classification: LCC PS3616.E5555 B625 2019 | DDC 813/.6—dc23
LC record available at https://lccn.loc.gov/2019019667

To Leila

NARRATOR'S NOTE:

What could be told of the stuff Bob do
began in one
and will be finished in two.
What can't be said
is shared in clue.
If you don't know stuff,
this is not for you.
There is no obfuscation of oratory,
simply a story told true,
with all the flexiloquence
of you know who.

CONTENTS

PRELUDE

When I was young I us'd to wait
On Massa and hand him de plate;
Pass down de bottle when he git dry,
And bresh away de blue tail fly...

TABANUS ATRATUS: blue tail fly. Common name: horsefly. A blue-black wing'ed bitch of a bloodsucker upon mammaldom. A harbinger of wasp fear, spreader of anthrax, and unindicted coconspirator to brave plantation slaves...

Jim crack corn and I don't care,
Jim crack corn and I don't care,
Jim crack corn and I don't care,
Ole Massa gone away.

Corn cracks as it goes through milling. Heads crack when pitched by horse into rocky ditch. Cracking corn, a colloquialism meaning gossip.

As the gossip goes, that song made so singularly popular by Burl Ives in 1964, and sung by schoolchildren in the valley of San Joaquin and valleys, villages, cities, and towns throughout the USA in the 1960s, had its roots in rebellion.

Den arter dinner massa sleep,
He bid dis niggar vigil keep;
An' when he gwine to shut his eye,
He tell me watch de blue tail fly.

Negro duties included thinning the swarms to keep their masters' horses from going skittish when ridden.

An' when he ride in de arternoon,
I foller wid a hickory broom;
De poney being berry shy
When bitten by de blue tail fly.
One day he rode aroun' de farm,
De flies so numerous dey did swarm;
One chance to bite 'im on the thigh,
De debble take dat blue tail fly.

It is said that the men 'round that particular *massa* conspired to bait the flies that his horse might humble him. Humble him it did. Cranium cracked and plashed on a pulverizing plantation stone.

De poney run, he jump an' pitch,
An' tumble massa in de ditch;
He died, an' de jury wonder'd why
De verdic was de blue tail fly.

Jim crack corn and I don't care,
Jim crack corn and I don't care,
Jim crack corn and I don't care,
Ole Massa gone away.

PART ONE

"Words are worthy of study."

—Corporal Earl Bligh

STATION ONE

UNBRANDED, UNBRIDLED, AND FREE

I N A TIME WHEN only the sane wear foil hats, a semblance of self-defense may have been a preferable
play by a man for whom the alliterative applications
to logic build barriers against mortal mourning. Still,
it would'a been a double-diorama to defend with all the
blood, brain, and brutal bits that Spurley's body had left
behind. It might also have been in Bob's mind that just
a splash of prosecutorial "lying in wait" jargon might'a
made their case and forced Bob to forever ferment in a
federal pen. He opted for fugitive flight, and the manhunt
immediately began, leaving doubt the duty of his most
diligent observers.

A search of the retirement home on the night of
Spurley Cultier's demise found Bob's bed magnificently
made, with tucks and folds that'd bring a Marine corps
drill instructor to drool in delight. Atop its trampoline-
tight duvet, an envelope fat with cash addressed to the

local ASPCA. No sign of Bob Honey, nor young Annie neither. Bob had commandeered Cultier's car from under the retirement home's most flowered tree, taking along his bald beauty to the rectory of an off-grid mountaintop monastery hidden amongst cathedral spires and dissimulative dispersion mists. There, within the damp quarry stone walls that Montenegrin masons made in a reach for the heavens, the FBI found her: Annie. Head in habit and honing Hebrews, her gaze seemingly steeped in some faraway fable, or perhaps fragile falsiloquence.

Sensing an agent's eyes of inquiry upon him, an ancient Athenian priest stood near in shadow, nodding affirmation of the poor girl's plight while another agent's interrogation of the girl sought any semblance of her remaining sanity. Robes may fool the fools, but even progressive Popes are politicians. By permission of the priest, they polygraphed her on site, but instead of it tracing truth from the peaks and valleys of graph, the machine went rogue, humming her witness with the virtuoso vibrations of von Bingen.[1] A cosmic event, this FD-302[2] was sure to be tucked away. To be safely secured from public scrutiny in the back of a bureau vault, where it might lie eternally deep in state. Catholic catatonia caged poor Annie's exculpatory rapture, leaving investigators singing psalms.

---

1   Hildegard von Bingen, the German Benedictine abbess composer and Christian mystic of the 1100s, composer of *Canticles of Ecstasy*.

2   FBI interview summary.

Some people do simply disappear.
They do it in marriages and they do it in fear.
They do it behind a brand.
They do it "going clear."
They do it growing old,
or as victim
at the blunt end
of a melee weapon…
While he will or he won't…Bob Honey don't.

He don't own anything of these aforementioned handicaps. Not anymore. Both man and mallet are out there; the Phil Ochs–favoring highwayman hiding in plain sight, drinking from our American aquifer, and howling his historic dreams toward Jupiter.

After riffle come the rapids
antsy intervals of river waves.
Normalized nihilism
Caustic current swirls
have caused a craze.
Advertisers claim the
drift Masters of right and wrong.
Religions cling
to mystic things
and all that's lasted far too long.
We thought Jesus crossed the Jordan
writing love in our love song.
So why's the choir singing
I'm incompatible with Christian thinking,
songs so petty, parsed, and weak

what is all this talk
of all this talk about a creep?
A swim in the New World river
Will it
dissuade one
of their God?
Is prayer the only way to him
in this his last unGodly nod?
Whirlpools whip and hydraulic surge
purging all who dare
Once, perfectly flawed mankind
Its package
an appeasement
to antiseptic underwear.
So little left distinguished
twixt public and private life
of man or woman,
the relinquished
danger is this man without a wife.
No norm
nor form,
I am…
The storm.

STATION TWO

THE GUN YARD

FROM THE GUN YARD come men of station, their voluntold tasks in forfeit of welcome to the wider world. Dogs of seething yearning deliver them to these, the kennels of resuscitation, before they stray. On the outer rim of this plot, what had years earlier touched the Uptown-most portion of the Twin Towers' debris field, the gun yard sits most often in the shadow of the Empire State Building in lower central Manhattan. A solitary city block of dilapidated eight-story structures connected by their improvised webs of cumberlanding wires,[3] so inexplicably unnoticed by passersby or developers' eye. Perhaps the pinnacle of permissive environments. Like people, some places go invisible to all but the wayward, and here in the age of anarchical whimsy, a full city block of significantly high-dollar real estate goes essentially unseen. Pedestrians pass, eyes on iPhones. Office workers of adjacent high-

---

3   Unauthorized tapping into powerlines.

rises barely browse above desktops, vaguely assuming the plot an old St. Aidan[4] housing project owned by a wealth without will to sell, develop, or refurbish. And those who inhabit it? The same who slip conventions of eye contact, toil in its shadowy solitude, and make their every entrance and exit by means of avoidance.

In quarters 6-H, a horsefly buzzes Bob brazenly for several minutes where he sits on a musty faux-Moroccan couch. This East Coast air is hot and thick and a looming storm is about to kick. In the soft amber light of a couch side lamp, a fly. It consistently collides, bumps, and bounces off both Bob's bare arms, a Japanese zero on a moon bounce.

ZZZT. Bump. ZZZT. Bump. ZZZT. Bump.

Then blackout.

Bob, initially thinking the power cut targeted him, accesses weapons and a night vision kit to counter the threat of encroachment. Once he's secured his sixth-floor safe house in a well-practiced series of praetorian protocols, he moves to observe through a peephole that the power cut reaches far down the streets, from spires of high-rise buildings to slabs of asundered avenues in an offset of the world's largest machine.[5] With threat assessment settled, he sets down his armaments, lights a small candle, and sits back down on the couch. The coming storm brings a deepening darkness that seems to amplify the buzzing, bouncing sound of this big-bodied old horsefly.

---

4   The patron saint of firefighters. He once saved a stag by making it invisible to hunters.

5   Power grid that blankets most of North America.

And the dull blades of gleeful guillotines,
had laughingly lopped his head
gavel to block, then spillage—
They might have thought him dead.
His body rises weary,
travels headless
ville to ville.
But he's not where the wind blows,
just inking up his quill.
His story far less heard
than hacked
and packed away
in a box labeled, 'lost and turd.'
He knew it would go that way
in the lessening
gradations of grays and gray.
From station to station
assault on alliteration.
From the cynical sensibilities
and assholes of sensation,
now let them scramble
to find what's lost
of their unimagined imagination.

Bob, not tone deaf, knows the primal screams of
toddlers and his country's own. Its notes of trauma state.
Women, men, conflation, confusion, tumult, and terror.
The one-ups and downs of Adam's desperation, and those
teeth of Lilith's swing. Eve has lost the poetic sheen of her
shine in shadow of Eden's stormy dome. Loosey-goosey talk

of predators, both real and imagined creditors. The outlaw's laughter from an adjacent room drifts under Bob's door like a prostitute's perfume. When the rare knock comes, it is the savior woman. A witchy old figure, she wears peanut butter in her brittle hair. She has corn-colored teeth, and a matted moldy muumuu covers her thickened knotty form. Some say she was once a dancer and that she'd given up the stage to raise Sri Lankan orphans, but then she got lost. Lost to this lair as the leprosy of her insides succumbs to the corrosion of Catholicism and the clever learned lure of adopting a cross to bear. Most in Bob's sector of the gun yard receive and revere her. They vouch for her wisdom, though it knows no saving grace for those she saves. Bob knows to ignore her knock, knows it's not really for him, and refuses witness to the hubris of her care.

Someone told a joke in 6-B. Jokes, Bob thinks, like treasure maps, each time told gain another recruit. All competing for the treasure of far-off hills and the whiff of pheromones that ensure pursuit. Expectations too high, aspirations too low. AM radio? The popular song is not music. Mr. Honey does not play well with others. The cold civil war is an inch from hot as he studies strategies from the gun yard. Mounds of data. City planning. Gas and electric. Water, power, robotics, magnets, mallet, and a peephole to spy the outerworld.

—

BOB NEVER WORE HIS hair too long. He liked it tidy, short, and clean. He'd shave whenever near a razor, with

or without cream. In times like these, when freedom ain't
free, he'd been called to grow it mid-back long along with
a burly beard of sedition. On outings, he'd go blackface,
smearing the meltings of telephone-pole tar deep into
skin and pores with his thickedy fingers to his face and
neck. He'd finish slathering his hands with the remaining
residue of his ink. Voila! A *jihadi* Jesus from the hood. He
wears a bathrobe over his clothes, figuring none would
look at what none could. Sidewalk sitters recite, "Get off
the cross, we need the wood." Only the homeless have
enough humor to engage in ad hominem heckles.

Black smoke from burning tires funnels upward
to the charcoal-powder midnight sky. In the absence of
ambient light—an atmospheric conversion in a turn of
the diurnal pattern, where sporadic explosive jets and
sprites of red and blue lightning dazzle and dare with the
intermittent classic bolt of white—he sees somersaulting
worlds of water sheeting down upon the gun yard and
throughout the surrounding city. Still, he sits in comfort
on the faux-Moroccan couch. The building shudders with
every meteorological boom. The horsefly perches in the
peephole, tremoring water from weary wings. Within
Bob's eyelet of overwatch, the dithering fly's building
buzzing claims claustrophobia in the quarter-bit hollow.
ZZZT! ZZZT! in Bob's ears until it seems to slowly mute
in Bob's mind. Sifting its vibration, his brain like the
surrounding storm suddenly overcome by the incoming
music of an ice cream truck. As Bob moves from couch
to peephole where the fly remains perched, all is suddenly

quite still. Bob leans in close to look below, careful his lash not wing the wing of the blue tail fly. The two of them there barely a hair's width apart, together looking down upon a street in torrent, where only snapping flashes of lightning might illuminate movement, and in a fix of flashes Bob and the horsefly watch a driverless ice cream truck float by. Inside of Bob, the irony. It is no longer he that is the drifting derelict vessel. Its inverter flickering a decorative string of colored bulbs where his anger toward exes drifts away. Though it has left the sightline of Bob and the fly, each holds its post. Only Bob's eyes shift to the fly. A staring standoff. Eye to eye. Man and fly. The fly plays tough guy—suddenly whirring a startling sustained buzz. Bob doesn't flinch. In such proximity its wings tickle his lash. On the fly's advance—SMASH! Human headbutts fly.

—

IN FULL FORCE, THE soporific storm is lulling the nation. For Bob, his own rest, similarly less *sleep* than semi-hallucinatory sedation. And in this hypnagogic state he remains perpetually on post, his visions cycling assessment scenarios of so many hyper-supposable threats to his security. REM rebounds near dawn in the wicked wild's worry dreams of all things gone. Tattooing a reticle on a ringleader's raccoon smirk whilst women of polished chrome wrest controls most contrived, and catastrophic cockfights make chicken-boys king until a pin of the new day's light pokes through the peephole, when Bob comes conscious in delirium. A growing feast of dreamlike images may threaten judgment and equilibrium. Yes, the brain will demand its sleep of Bob while Bob gets up and does his job.

—

THE MORNING IS SUNNY and still. Drippings fall from high and low sills. Gutters stream, puddles plop deep, but life goes on after the prior night sky's worrisome weep. Now, in hallucinatory deprivation and eccentric black masquerade, Bob takes his daily walk. A slight whisper of sound from an even slighter whisper of trees. It is not music Bob hears. Not the trees of Woodview that sang his working-class soul to tears, those from choirs of branch, leaf, or pine needles in serenade. Nor was it the grating circus music of an ice cream truck selling out the far-gone fabric of femininity. Not that. No. These barren trees hush notes on stave—notes composed December 8, 1980, by Chapman's hand, gun, and broken mind—and deliver the ricocheting echoes from Seventy-Second Street.[6] Trees that seem to masturbate an ejaculation of wounds wishing and longing for Lennon's laments, so lost to Bob in his losing of Woodview's familiar contentments or tolerances. The daily piercing of this big apple. Under his feet he feels the subway system's rumble, where even his love of trains could not come for free. Pricey stuff in a kakistocracy...

yet only three hours by train
is Washington, DC.

---

6   Reference to the building where John Lennon was shot and killed.

STATION THREE

THE CHASER OR THE CHASTE

I T CAN BE A pickle to sort a predisposition from a premonition, a fickle folly from a formidable phrase, or a pursuer from the pursued. While the FBI continued casting wide nets in their collection scheme, angling for actionable intelligence, a more nefarious network of public/private enterprises and agencies were acting on instinct in their pursuit of Bob. Unbound by warrants or other constitutional inconveniences, this parallax army, the men and women for whom sacraments of special weapons and tactics is their sanctioning to blindness in battle, have been led to succumb to a myth of higher calling, and with their own voluntary self-righteous numbing of individualism, enter a dynamic where they are empowered by an empathy scorned, and enabled by their master's willful suppressions of consciousness, where any nod to the value of human life finds bypass. In this ire of imperial impunity comes a painted landscape of warfare from a palette of

such luscious acrylic lethality, that its vibrancy of brilliant-
ly kaleidoscopic colors dazzle a Louvre more expeditious
than any commoner's rule of law may exhibit. Salem and
McCarthy had given witch hunts a bad name, and not until there were more interracial couples in ads for vacations
than actually exist throughout all the nations did we come
to identify the real among witches worthy of fire. Was Bob
Honey among those heretics? When did an idealized reality take lead over real life's representation?

In the parallax view, defects and disorders of personality present at premium purchase. And here, where trea-
son's child is born of a mercilessly murdered man, comes a
compliment of predisposition to measures most unsound,
unsavory, and seemingly undefeatable. Hence, a certain
tolerance would be extended to the intermittent bout of
personalization. Still, red flags demand monitoring. The
algorithms that hotlist hot tempers, may they stray:

MEMORANDUM

FROM: The Office of the Deputy Director of █████████
CLASSIFICATION: HIGHLY CLASSIFIED
DISTRIBUTION DATE: █████████

This memo is not for distribution and intended for use by
members of the █████████ and designated █████████
USG officials only.

SUBJECT: Project Rogue

THREAT LEVEL: HIGH

MEANS OF RECOVERY: Triggered autonomous internal hotlist cyber monitors. Intercepted prior to distribution.

To: Mr. Robert Honey

RE: ████████████████████████

Sender: ████████████████████

Mr. Honey—

In the accepted morality of our shared country is a great strength and resiliency to absorb and accept the collateral damages necessary to maintain the values of our capitalist orientation. I am neither a man of vendetta nor the virulence of liberalism. I write you today neither as the ████████████ slaughtered, nor as the willing functionary of your demise, though I am both. I write instead as a born girl who grew up with a love for hunting and the outdoors. I think I know a few things about prey, and I've been sniffing your track for some time now. Like you, I hold myself to a very high professional standard. I have honed my skills on multiple hunts and kills, and it occurred to me that I may strengthen my physical stature in such a way to improve my skill sets exponentially. With copious intake of intramuscular testosterone, and our modern era's most sophisticated means of gender reassignment, am I today no longer the ██████ I was born, but the ██████ I was born to be. You, my friend, are to me little more than a rat moving through the crawlspaces of this, our American life, cheating us of the cheese that is rightly ours. I have a taste for rats and an ethic to eat all parts of my prey. I will take you, and when I do, I'll butcher you

into bits of size to feed my Cuisinart. I'll then transfer
each pulpy ounce of your body into a bucket. I'll whisk
you. Then I'll cook you like fluffy eggs in bacon grease.
I'll eat every bit and bite of you. I know the kind of man
you are. The disaffected, disingenuous. A man whose
only alibi is his ability to organize chaos and bring chaos
to clarity. A man whose moral code knows only the
odious. You are an embittered misogynist masquerading
as a murderer in search of love. I will make you love
me, Mr. Honey, and then I will humiliate you. I am a
patient hunter and a perfect marksman, but you, I will
take by blade in Baltimore. Big game or small, it's all the
same to me. I'm still so fond of little pink dresses, the
bounce of my daddy's knee, the memories of the child
that I used to be. Somehow, and I don't know why, you
remind me of a postman, a mail carrier who worked the
neighborhood of my youth. There was a dodginess of
his darting eyes that disturbed me. I said, "Daddy, the
mailman disturbs me." For my fifth birthday, I was given
five of his fingers from his favored hand. From that
time on, just watching him deliver with his left gave me
delight. That my father left the rest of him intact was
an order of mercy. Something he kindly kept from my
own nature. I'll be seeing you someday in Baltimore and
we'll do our little dance, won't we?

Sincerely,

███████████████

ANALYSIS and RECOMMENDATION:
Agent ████–057 should remain project lead until further
notification. As the memo was written but unsent, and with

no evidence that Agent ███████-057 is currently in possession or has knowledge of SUBJECT ROGUE whereabouts, agency should continue monitoring. NOTE: There is a mention of the city of Baltimore that we currently suspect to be non-literal. Neither subject nor pursuer have any known connections to the city in Maryland. In addition, the agent's reference to "fluffy eggs and bacon grease" would constitute disclosure of sources and methods had the memo been shared with subject. We will continue to track.

STATION FOUR

A BODY IN BOWERCHALKE TURNS[7]

Bob enters the Greek Grill, a diner for the down-and-out on the periphery of the gun yard. The place is empty but for one older black gentleman who sits at the far end of the counter. Bob sits at the near. A young Greek-American server wears a sloganed T-shirt, Use Your Delusions printed across chest and belly. Bob orders scrambled eggs, crisp bacon, white toast, and a side dick of death[8] (charred). The old man at the far end is pocketing small foil-wrapped slabs of butter from a communal customer dish, occasionally checking traffic for the waiter's eye. But Bob watches him, and when the man catches Bob's gander, he smiles conspiratorially before standing from his stool and moving slyly to the back of the diner and into the men's room. Bob sees his coffee before him, and in its reflection his own black and bearded face.

---

7   Resting place of author William Golding.

8   Military slang for sausage.

The increasing wrinkles around his eyes assuring him that he is fifty-seven and getting no younger...

WHOOSH!

Suddenly six years old, Bob is retroactively white and in his first-grade classroom. His teacher is slender and pretty, too pretty to teach a six-year-old with premature inclinations of erotica. But on this day, Ms. Winer's got something better than her body for six-year-old Bobby. She's demonstrating the dynamics of a rudimentary pulley system. *Creak, creak, creak.* She pulls the line over the roller, lifting a thirty-pound[9] weight from the floor. But, as each of the students watches the rope roll over the roller, Bob sees something different. He sees the roller rolling over the line. The teacher calls for the kids to queue up in front of the weight. Each takes a turn squatting down to lift the weight with their own hands. Some get it higher than others. Some don't get it up at all. They giggle and mock each other, but Bob's eye stays on the pulley. Now the children line up on the line-side of the pulley and each in turn succeeds in wonder as they leverage weight from floor—even, yes *even*, the girls.

FLASH!

It's the very next day of school. Ms. Winer stands before her class. She's not looking so obviously sexy to Bob today, she's looking rather stern. Something he'd come to pursue of women too many times in the adult life that would

9   Thirty pounds average to the max weight a six-year-old could lift of their own accord.

follow. Yes, Ms. Winer is looking very stern today and Bob is nursing a swollen ankle. "Yesterday," she tells the class, "we all had fun and got to experiment with the pulley and the weight, but something very dark happened before the end of the school day, something very mischievous. One of you—yes, one of your schoolmates here in this class—stole the pulley."

A group gasp escapes the children, but not Bob, himself an early master of the "it wasn't me" face.

"Now," says Ms. Winer, "would the young lady or gentleman who stole the pulley like to confess?" She scans the silent class. Each student looking more unwittingly guilty than the next. Her eyes lock on Bob and the excellent expression of innocence that separates only him from the others. "Mr. Honey?"

"Yes, Ms. Winer?"

"I'm a good judge of character, young man, and I'm proud to say that you are indeed a young man of character. Tomorrow, class, I am going to ask that the thief return the pulley, and my deputy Mr. Honey and I will break you up into two groups, each supervised by one of us." She points to wooden storage cupboards on opposing walls behind the students. "Each group will line up in front of those cupboards. One at a time, you will go into the cupboard, and if it's Mr. Honey's cupboard, you will have an opportunity in Mr. Honey's cupboard, and in the privacy of closed cupboard doors, to reach to the upper shelf and slide the pulley where it will be out of reach or sight of others to the back of the upper shelf.

As soon as one student comes out, another of you will go in. Then, the one who first went in will walk quickly to my cupboard, where you will have a second opportunity to return the pulley, in just the same manner. If at the end of this exercise, neither cupboard's shelf has the returned pulley on it, I will be speaking to your parents. Each and every one of them. Because there is not one among you who I cannot offer some disciplinary advice for. Are we understood?"

The students, despite their terror and confusion, murmur a polite, "Yes, Ms. Winer."

"Now, the last thing I want to ask before we go on with Tom and Jane: can anyone in this class tell me why one of your fellow students would want a pulley so badly that they would commit this crime?"

Bob raises his hand.

"Yes, Bob."

"Because they don't know how dangerous they are."

For a moment, Ms. Winer as well as Bob's fellow students believe he's serious, but then upon realizing he's telling a joke, they all begin to giggle—even Ms. Winer.

FLASH!

It's yesterday after school, Bob has twisted a thin line of cable around the horizontal post of a short green vinyl-coated chain-link fence. He tightens the bind with a pair of pliers. He runs the other end of the cable line up to a high post of his tree house, about a forty-five-foot span at 0.436 radian. He is positioning the pulley on the high end of the line. He has fastened the handle bars of a Schwinn

Stingray to the pulley, and standing atop his tree house, he readies himself for a ride across the line.

He shoves off. At six, Bob has not calculated the ratio of his body weight to the line's tension. What he thought the greatest hazard, or otherwise catastrophic system failure with velocity repression stopper and his then inevitable impact with the garden-green chain-link—will not come to pass. Within a fraction of a second after shoving off, his body plummets in a sudden, direct freefall to ground some twelve feet below.

—

THE WRINKLES AROUND HIS blackened eyes return as he sips his coffee. The old fella returns to his stool under Bob's suspicious eye, rolls up his sleeves, takes one butter packet out of his pocket at a time, unwrapping and warming its yellow cube between his hands and proceeding to rub it up and down his arms like lotion. He catches Bob's gaze. The old man speaks. His southern black drawl, "Don't tell the Greek, but I come here to use the worshroom. When a black man use soap, his skin dry ashen. You was wonderin' bout da *butta*, am I right?"

Bob answers, "I was, yes."

"Come on down 'ere," says the old man. "Sit ba'me."

Bob reluctantly appeases, taking a stool beside the old man.

The Greek exits the kitchen with eggs, bacon, and white toast, places it by Bob, then regards the old man. "You gonna order something?"

"I'm gonna order what I already got in my gullet," replies the old man. "I still got a half'a cup left."

"You can't stay here all day with one cup of coffee. You finish your coffee and get moving or order something."

"I'll do that. I'll finish my coffee," says the old man. The Greek is skeptical but makes his way back to the kitchen.

"I'm Wilbert Gulpton, Bob," blurts the old fella.

"You know me?" asks Bob.

"Ahh," draws the old man. "What kin I say? I sees, I hears, I scribbles, and you? You do what I say you do."

"I do what you say I do?"

"Even the free gotta serve sumbudy… Me now? I wadn't always a free man, ma' own se'f. Se-enteen year ol', they grab me up on two charges. One. Grand larceny. Stealin' tires—DIDN'T do dat. Two. Statutory rape—sho' DID do dat. That little piece a shuga wawv' woorf it. Halloween nineteen seventy-two. I trick'a treat da girl next doh. She appear. Offa' me sympathetic smile. Den, angle huh eyes to a pile'a candy on the floh, she say, 'You stay here, you can only have one. You leave, you can have foh.' I took one…and went in the doh. Sixteen years on a chain gang in Angola Penitentiary."

Gulpton breaks into song:

> *Oh, we call the sun ol' Hannah*
> *Blazing on my head*
> *Yes, we call the sun ol' Hannah*
> *And her hair is flamin' red.*
> *Why don't you go down, ol' Hannah*
> *Don't you rise no more*

If you come up in the mornin'
Bring judgment sure
Bring judgment sure

Kept sayin' I was a good man
But they drove me down
Yes, I was a good man,
But they drove me down
Well, it look like ev'rything
Ev'rything I do
Yes, it looks like ev'rything
Ev'rything I do...
is wrong.

He grabs a couple more foil-wrapped butter slabs for the road, pockets them.

"See ya got ya self cozy over there in that gun yawd. I think it's about time," says the old man to Bob, "that I offer to advance your skills in illusion."

"My skills in illusion."

The two men catch themselves looking into each other's faces when the old man suddenly smiles and says, "You know me."

"No sir."

"That's right," says the old man.

"And who are you? You're Wilburt Gulpton."

"You," says the old man.

"Me?"

"Me."

And again, "Me?" questions Bob.

"We met down there in San Antonio, before you got yourself in all that trouble. You're looking at my face. Let me show you something." The old man lifts his finger to his eye and peels away a tiny flap of black-skinned lid, exposing the white skin beneath.

Bob is dazzled. "That's what I mean," says the old man. "Skills of illusion. Nobody thinks you're black. And don't mistake me as a promoter of precious pregnant pause experts or the pious. I speak of a craftsman in the fine art of camouflage. Mockery is midget-minded misunderstanding. We—men like you and I—have a job to do, and we will employ tactics unappealing for the better good. You just look like a crazy white guy with tar all over his face. I'm not saying that's without value, I'm just noticing that you're working too hard. You don't have to try and do it so perfect-like when it's never going to look like I do."

"The storyteller?" asks Bob. "Pappy...?"

"Pariah—but let's not focus on the mundane. Leave that to the Micronesians and the matron you might meet at a cake bake in Sharm El-Sheikh. Now close your crumb-catcher and hear what I've got to say. Everybody's got a campaign—what's yours, Bob Honey with a bullet in his head? If you understand water, you understand the world. Don't be like most fellas and girls making themselves up like a teacup in a waterfall. It will limit your retention. This water is not falling for catch and release. You wanna stand back from that waterfall so it can be caught by all your cups—sealed, replenished, and retained. Collect and keep. Collect and keep. Collect and keep. What's branding?"

"Being?" questions Bob.

"Now you're on track," says Pappy. "The Acela Express runs from Penn to DC's Union Station in three hours ride time. The International Space Station orbits the planet in ninety-two minutes. REM sleep generally takes an hour to achieve and I've got exactly six seconds before a man from an island in the Mediterranean Sea gives a proper preacher from Appalachia the boot."

With that comes the Greek from the kitchen. "You! You finish your coffee. You pay. You go."

The old man reaches into his pocket. Bob lifts his tar-covered hand in gesture to stop him. Reaches into his own pocket and pulls out a couple of one-dollar bills and throws them on the counter between the old-timer and the Greek. "I'll pay for his coffee," Bob says.

"Thank you kindly, young man," says the old-timer. "Thank you kindly." He stands, pats Bob on the back, and exits the diner.

"Six ninety-five," blurts Bob.

"Six ninety-five?" asks the Greek.

Bob pulls exactly a five, a one, and ninety-five cents change from his pocket in one pull. Complements the two bills that he paid out for Pappy. "That's what I owe you for breakfast," Bob says.

"You pay no tip?" asks the Greek.

"Kindness is my tip. Try it next time my friend comes in."

As Bob stands and walks toward the door, from behind him, the Greek calls out, "Kindness? What you know about kindness?"

With one blackened hand opening the door, this stops Bob. He turns back to the Greek.

"That it can be a very harsh thing."

—

UPON RETURN TO THE gun yard, Bob hears buzzing above. He crosses the yard beneath the web of wires welching from the grid. He steps onto the exterior stairwell, pauses as he follows his ears and sees the amassing of horseflies on the wall outside where the peephole peeks from his sixth-floor quarters. He lumbers slowly upward as the buzzing builds. He enters on the sixth-floor landing, closes a heavy door behind him, and walks the corridor to his quarters. Key in door. He opens it. Again, he can hear the buzzing through the peephole and now sees one brave blue tail scout fluttering in through the hole. Bob steps halfway toward it, stopping midway through the room. He watches as the scout fly studies the splattered body of his fallen comrade, crushed by Bob's head the evening before. The quiet scout looks to Bob, and Bob eyes the scout. Without warning, the buzzing accelerates as one after another, the scout welcomes each among the swarm of soldiers to enter through the peephole and into the room. Bob watches as they coalesce in observance of their fallen splattered comrade. Buzzing buddies in briefing chatter. While their utterances are a bit pesty, Bob employs an intuit to interpret:

> "What d'ya think?/ What do I think?/I
> think that's the guy—that guy in the

middle of the room./ He's the guy?/ That
guy right there...?/ You think that guy
right there killed Amos?/ Fuck Amos—he's
a fuckin' horsefly./ What do you think you
are, shorty?/ Come on, fellas, concentrate!/
So that's the guy that killed Amos? Hey
ho—the witch is dead."

And so it go. The banter of blue tail flies. Time for
deployment. The swarm widens on the wall around the
peephole, single-filing from exterior to in, a spreading out
on entry like a water stain on a blanket. This deployment
of flies spreads until they fill the far wall, then expands in
numbers to floor, ceiling, walls left and right. There is only
space for Bob's feet, now surrounded by a floor of buzzing
horseflies as the spreading swarmage coats the wall of
the entry door behind him. He is surrounded by a wall-
to-floor and floor-to-ceiling cocoon of flies. The buzzing
intensifies. He hears their lies. *"Our God, our God, take us*
forth to war." The mass of these undulating insects, like
viscous liquid in a delicately tipping dish. A near hypnosis
comes to Bob, in the coal-wall glimmer cast by the arterial
structures of wings. The oval bubbles of their blue-black
bodies with eyes of uncertain death and patterns of
purgatory in postulations of pain. The burden is on Bob to
give freedom to flies. He is their God. He is God.

STATION FIVE

HONEYSUCKLE ROSE

SWARMS OF FLIES OR redheads, real or imagined, are not new to Bob. Yet the more intensely these visits weigh upon his consciousness, the more inclined he finds himself to get up, get on, and just do stuff. His has been a life not so much rooted in reality as one where the workings of his imagination and otherwise detrimental deprivation of sleep affirm themselves in eventualities. A collection of hindsights proven real of retroactive prophecy. Waking dreams that have come to fruition. It was at a very young age that Bob learned to turn and face fears, that no phantom might take him from behind.

In 1969, he and a gaggle of neighborhood kids saw fit to scrawl REDRUM in mud on the house next to Bob's own. The family who lived there was on an outing that day, but kids bein' kids, Bob and his vanguard of valley vandals overindulged the crime scene in admiration of their handiwork, and the family returned recognizing Bob

and the other local kids as they fled. The Gurshlaugs were
German, the father a fright; his paraplegic body, confined
to an early model electric wheelchair, had the monstrous
air of a Reichstag robot. Though seldom heard, his harsh
voice and German accent cut through the neighborhood
like a Nazi knife set.

It seemed to young Bob that whatever had placed
Mr. Gurshlaug in that chair had left him to a boundless
bitterness, and from that bitterness had been born a
monster. Mrs. Gurshlaug offered little more charm than
her husband as she informed Bob's parents of his misdeed.
She had rapped on the family's front door, and when Bob's
mother opened it, a drooling-spitting Mrs. Gurshlaug
demanded in a tirade of spit-addled speech that Bob's
father whip him with a belt from her own supply.

In humiliation and terror, young Bob was instead
forced to power-hose the REDRUM from the side of the
Gurshlaug home under the seething eye of the robotic
Nazi and his drooling hausfrau. In addition, Bob was given
a three-day grounding and confined in his room to busy
himself with Silly Putty, Slinky, and a sadomasochistic
magazine secured on a past Sunday's scavenger hunt.

On the fourth day, finally free, Bob sat on the roof of
his family's chicken coop, taking in the clucks and manic
movements of poultry pets. The Gurshlaug yard sat behind
the chicken coop, separated from Bob's by a six-foot fence
swallowed by a boisterous hedge of honeysuckle. Bob
could move from the hard-surfaced chicken coop roof
to the couch-like overgrowth, and while sitting atop the

hedge, Bob got lost in the taste of honeysuckle nectar and the music of clucking chickens. He'd pulled one after another of the tubular flowers through his teeth while hummingbirds suckled the same in a close and trusting proximity. Bob liked animals and animals liked Bob. So lost in the day's sunshine and delicate buzzing of bees was Bob that it all conspired to lull him to sleep while sitting up straight. In that moment of slumber, his equilibrium on pause, Bob tipped, dropping into German territory on the far side of the honeysuckle hedge. As if on cue, from a corrugated tool shed, the sudden and unfortunate presence of Mr. Gurshlaug in battery-charged chair. The buzzing of the chair's motor, the shift of its turn—*Zzzt! Zzzt! Zzzt!*—and by the time Bob looked up, ghoulish old Gurshlaug was barreling straight for him. *Zzzzzzzzz!* "VHAT ARE YOU DOINGK IN MY YAWT!? ZIS IS NOT YOUR PROPERTY! I KILL YOU!"

In energy sciences, Flea Power refers to residual static electricity on electrical components after switch-off, but what few know of real fleas is the power of their jump, which can catapult them as high as thirty-eight times their body length with an acceleration so intense they may withstand one hundred G's, whereas the average human is rendered unconscious by five to six. It takes about one one-thousandth of a second for a flea to hurl itself into the air. What is most extraordinary about this is that the energy generation necessary is one hundred times more power than their muscles can actually provide. It all comes down to a stretchy protein called resilin instantaneously released to the springlike tissues of their muscles. Bob boy went flea that day and found himself in flight over the honeysuckle hedge into his own yard, landing on his feet before fleeing in mortal fear. Halfway through the yard, he seized and came to a most sudden stop. Something deep inside him had shifted. A current of something cathartic shuddered through his body. Why am I running? Why am I afraid? What could he really do to me? Why not stop and throw rocks at the paraplegic? Why not laugh and taunt him, shifting side to side too quickly for his chair to respond?

He would never run away from fear again. It's net negative to survival. The cowardice of its clammy hands hoodwinks us into the translation of fear as danger. There was no danger at his door. No danger in REDRUM. No danger in DC.

No danger where there is opportunity.

—

To THE WESTERN EAR, the Vietnamese language can sound short, with starts of unprovoked hostility. At the Grand Central Station–adjacent Moonflower Beauty and Nail Salon, a gaggle of jackhammer-voiced Saigon stowaways shout out insufferable gossip and direction. Bob's legs and arms are waxed, nails mani-ed and pedi-ed, his face steamed, shaven, and moisturized. His lashes tinted and pride tainted, but the job is the job and this one is for Bob.

"You pay me mo' money!" demanded the proprietor, Min. "I have take off blackface. I tell people you have blackface, dey make you bad. You want no be bad man, you pay me mo' money."

Bob reaches into his sock for socked-away cash.

"Mo'," says Min.

"It's enough," says Bob. "My face wasn't black, it was telephone-pole tar. Take the money or tell who you like." With a curtsy, Bob thanks the gaggle and exits the salon.

—

AT THE PLUS-SIZE PROPRIETARY Dress Barn, Bob adorns his body in casual chic topped by a floral-sequined scarf meant to mask the increasing turkey skin of his thickening neck. Next, he's off to wig up at Lady Day Wigs NYC, whose poster child is Raquel Welch. Once wigged and bespectacled, Bob is weddy for travel. Inside his head, as he hits the street, he can't help but hear Harry Nilsson sing:

Everybody's talkin' at me
I can't hear a word they're sayin',
Only the echoes of my mind

He saunters along the sidewalk, a quick study in the ways of the kind of women who warble. In the clutches of discomfort comes the comfortable sounds of trains. Bob is on track, resembling Madalyn Murray O'Hair.[10] Having boarded the train at Penn station, he feels the liberation of being on the run with a face so undistinguishable as his

---

10   Founder of the American Atheists movement. Murray O'Hair was most noted for having brought prayer in school to a close. She was rewarded for her characteristic charmlessness by being murdered by a close friend.

has become. Where the world's caution of a man is without prosaic patience and its loathing for him blinding and misguided. It doesn't take a tough skin to obligate man to mission. It is said that the toughest guy on the block is the one with the least to lose. Bob is God's most liberated man, a pariah to the anarchy attached to his optics. Convenient, the mallet in Margaret's purse.[11]

—

THERE ARE CERTAIN JOYS in life that, once had, never leave a man's desire: the sweet licorice of blue-wrapped Blackjack gum, the coveted clovey flavor-burst of Beeman's in red and white, or the wax-paper-wrapped maple bars made fresh in the wee hours at Helms Bakery, the delivery trucks of which young Bob would give chase to for breakfast. But in nothing and nowhere does Bob find such satisfaction as in the seat of a sixty-five-ton passenger car riding the rails of evasion and escape. There is something in the intoxication of trains, in their rumble, romance, and fatherly muscularity. The solitary serenity of their sensation that defies explanation. For Bob, it is just so simply soothing. Get outside his invisible peace, and the faces of fellow passengers' eyes are so seemingly participant to a paranoia unbecoming of passengers. Their trappings of false icons and exploitation of confectionary religion, parental judgments, the sorcery of social media, and the consuming and looming consumption of the Fourth Estate. Not Bob. He keeps his pursuers real as the rabid dogs of the gun yard. He lives

---

11   A costumed tactical bag.

free of fear knowing he can turn on a dime and bite back at beasts, however bold. He can liquidate a libertine and turn a mallet to a spire. He's on fire.

—

His prophecy of pursuers has served him well. Back in his gun yard abode, Bob—through a peephole— observes his fellow renegades now under siege. Two black helicopters hover above. Paramilitaries sweep building to building, room to room, clearing, cuffing, and gunning down those who resist. The savior woman assuming ascent takes angel's flight from a rooftop. Whoops. DROP.

From an invisible wasteland and bastion of apostasy and pity, the gun yard is revealed, bangity bangity-bang. There is dueling in this latter-day Dodge City. A new sheriff just been brought, and the trail runnin' hot. Marshaling the paramilitaries is an imposing transgender agent, his face, it seems to Bob, a patchwork from harvested human tissue. His heavy breath animating an animal's hunger for particular prey. His entry team radios from above: "Sir, we have 6-H surrounded, are we clear to make entry?"

As outside, something soars unseen, the agent replies, "Hold position. I'm going live."

"Copy."

Across the street, two sanitary engineers have locked another dumpster to the loading fork of their truck. They pause to observe the gun-yard sideshow. The driver hits its hydraulics and the fork raises the dumpster, but the volume of its hoist distracts from the show and before completing its drop, the truck's driver stops it, leaving it suspended in midair. He too wants to hear what's going on over there. From the gun yard, the paramilitary PA squawks as the agent speaks.

"Mr. Honey, this is raid command! You have one minute to surrender peacefully. In that minute, you will remove all clothing and exit into the corridor on your belly, hands and fingers extended fully forward. The one-minute countdown commences immediately."

Inside the dumpster, a fresh falafel wrapper stamped with the Greek Grill logo drifts amongst the collected gutter garbage. Suddenly, the cracking of automatic rifle fire confirming building entry has been made. A fast-rope team drops from helicopter to rooftop, sets themselves to repel the building's façade. Yo-yo men make swinging ingressions through the windows of all floors. One trooper inadvertently finds something squishy under his boot. The sole of it, and all his weight, have stumbled on the body of a dead infant. He moves with the others on approach to 6-H. The chopper swoops and horseflies swarm. Rabid dogs wrangled, ferocious fat felons flex-cuffed, and wistful women lost are found.

Not Bob. Bob is Margaret, flown the coop by concoction of cable.

Now at safe distance, we've found him, a liberated woman on a train.

The raid commander arrives at 6-H. His strike team dejected and fearing his wrath as he wanders the empty room. Kicks and curses in the clutter of maggots born.

At mission's end, the garbage truck driver reboots the hydraulic-loading fork of his dumpster to continue its rise until a loud metallic CLANG from above. He shuts it down, steps outside the truck, following the gaze of his two sanitary engineers. The dumpster has collided with the handlebars of a bicycle fixed to pulley and cable zipline, its near end fastened to a telephone pole above and beside the truck. Their eyes follow the cable backward, all the way up to its connection on the exterior of quarters 6-H.

"Damn, boy!"

Bob's trumpet sounds:

> *The bombs fall on St. Christopher*
> *across the Aegean Sea.*
> *Where oh where, oh where,*
> *is credibility?*
> *Parkland kids, a sign of hope,*
> *But opiate families can barely cope*
> *in the reign of terror and pharmaceutical dope.*
> *Iran glares at America*
> *in fabled Friday prayer,*
> *they'd better pray a little bit more*
> *now in US strategic crosshair.*
> *Beauty, birth, and private things*
> *if unbranded do not show.*
> *Yet they are all that's real, aren't they*
> *of all we'll ever know.*
> *As the virtue signalers sanctify synchronicity,*
> *raising ratings for their shows.*

STATION SIX

A WHINNY AND A WHINNY AND A HA-HA-HA

WOMEN ARE SMARTER THAN men and they don't play fair," or so had said a wizened cowboy in young Bobby's ear. As life lived on, and Bob played his hand at sex and courtships, more often than not, those western words offered calming mercies in otherwise chaotic interludes of incursion on his crimson heart. It can be said that a woman's greatest weakness comes as a result of denying her own truth, and perhaps, as was Bob's view, this was a more sympathetic Achilles' heel than that which plagued manhood—that hardwired con on boys to believe their own lie, sportin' Stetson, plaid, Levi's, and shades. Somewhere in the system is a DID,[12] and the design of its delay is unique to each individual and their hunger to evolve a personal originality that might otherwise be baked in. If discovering harmony, intimacy, play, peace, and support between brands of estrogen and testosterone

---

12   Delayed Ignition Device.

were on any male's menu of priority consumptions, one would have to take it in little bites and chew slowly per the doctor's recommendation. But this, like Highway 50 from Colorado to California deemed "the loneliest highway in America," was a ride of contradictions too little known to the average camper. Bob was a camper both commercial and clandestine throughout the American west, the Middle East, North and sub-Saharan Africa, and most importantly American motels he'd found in towns sung about by the troubadours that touched the chapters of his soul's search by ride, rail, and the thumb stuck out. Then, somewhere along that tinker's trail, a surrender to the value of one's own flesh, bones, and bulwark.

In the reconciliation of roaming relativity, once were women who took and even boasted reluctant joy in the whistles of Romans like rites of passage. From within this rank and file's finesse had come the confidence that would uninhibit him of his inhibitions to male/female discourse. Peaked, he deemed himself ready for the dame of his desire. Unexpected was that she would come to him in the form of a chubby, *I Love Lucy*–haired lass.

—

TO BOB, SHE OPENED her box of evanescent entries and exits as though it were a caring thing. He bought her stocks while his were on the rise. "Buy," she said, and buy he did, until access to her pussy crashed with the market. All day trading had been traded away. She'd not cum to stay, but rather to practice coy charms in another's arms. She'd

asked Bob about himself, assuming her interrogatories a
flattering curiosity. It would not be her last misread of Bob,
nor her last expression of ostentation's overconfidence.

—

A TURNING POINT IN Bob's marriage took place when
on their wedding day, his now ex-wife wondered if Bob
might be questioning their vows. There was, she said,
a transparency of reluctance in his expression. "Why
doubt?" she asked.

To this he responded, "It's a good question. Or do you
mean it philosophically?"

In seeming sanctimony, it was she now slow to respond,
and in that beat of her abeyance, Bob silently filled various
blanks in his continued response: the mailman, the red-
haired muff, and her constant reconstitution of cosmetics
with ever-ready powder puff. The distractions at a day's
end dominated by her readership of Google alerts to the
activities of soccer players.

Serving as best man, Jann Scitelli, a Western Test Range
colleague of Bob's, intervened in the awkward stall before
the magistrate and moved the vows to conclusion. Remote
at best had been Scitelli's relationship with Bob, and he
was quick to leave the awkward service the moment the
marriage had been pronounced. "See you at work, Bob."

"Yes, Jann. At work."

Guests of the affair included the women of what his
new wife called her "family," a sycophantic cadre under
the redhead's command. They had formed the Woodview

Women's Entrepreneurial Co-Op, which later led them to prime staff positions in the ice cream company of their doyen. Also in attendance, uninvited: Bob's uncle Craig, who'd flown in from Fairbanks. A former military man, Craig's battle wounds had saddled him with a left-side lazy mouth and a propensity to spontaneous vulgarity. He'd spent much of the ceremony targeting the magistrate with a mumbled "cocksucker!" A muttering just loud and constant enough to leave his involuntary listeners inured. Finally, there was Albert Locklear, who ran the Woodview Lumber and Hardware. Bob was a regular browser and buyer in the store's aisles and invited Albert on a whim. It was also Albert in whom Bob confided to aid in the selection of a honeymoon destination, as Albert's expertise included two failed marriages.

When Bob and his bride arrived at the Pechanga Resort Casino in Temecula, near Lake Elsinore, Bob pridefully outstepped the doorman to lead his new bride to the concierge desk, where a young man in a tailored suit read from a script pre-provided by Bob.

"Hello, Mr. Honey. Mrs. Honey." He passed them two room keys and a mini map in a sleeve. "I'm sure Mr. Honey will have no trouble following the resort map to your room. There is an amenity waiting for you." Now paraphrasing, the young man meandered. "We were able to upgrade you to a king suite. We've gone ahead and booked your balloon tour for tomorrow morning. You can pick up the shuttle in our traffic circle at seven a.m." To Bob's dismay, the young man goes off-script completely. "Mr. Honey, I knew

you'd want to let Mrs. Honey avail herself of the Outlets
at Lake Elsinore tomorrow afternoon. And, Mrs. Honey,
you'll enjoy Williams Sonoma, the Nike Factory Store,
and both Van Heusens and Sketchers are holding a
sale. The Outlets are a personal favorite extravagance
of mine." As the young man continued his pitch, Uncle
Craig's voice begins building in Bob's head. "Cocksucker-
cocksucker-cocksucker."

Unlike cancer, where cell structures multiply and
divide, conversations of retail outlets put the construction
of those cells supporting Bob's socialization in rapid
decline. Blood vessels rushed north to oxygenate his
brain just as he might soon need them south for the
consummation of a marriage that would consume him.
Once between the sheets of the king suite's bed and faced
with the chubby redhead's horse-like heaving, Bob found
himself finally married and officially alone.

While Bob could summon something of an erection
at the mere notion of a naked woman, sustaining sex
without rushing ejaculation meant playing mind games
in order to distract his impatience. There in that room at
the Pechanga Resort Casino, he whittled away at his wife's
whinny with compartmentalization of that which made
her most appear a woman.

A woman.

And what was it in a woman that made her not a man?

STATION SEVEN

COCK-A-DOODLE-DO

INTRODUCING MURRAY WATERMAN. THE formerly sitting senator seems to have found his seat amongst the proletariat. He picks up the train in Baltimore and, just as it is about to lunge forward, relaxes his ass adjacent to Bob's Margaret. As people are prone to do when scanning their new surroundings, Bob and Murray catch each other's eye. Bob recognizes this public man. He chooses to clue Murray with a manufactured wink. Murray smiles. "How do you do, ma'am?"

And, in falsetto, says Bob, "I'm well, thank you."

Murray opens his Mac and does whatever business a former senator sitting on several boards and consultancies may do. Bob ponders Murray's malady. A pathogenic potpourri of poor judgments that often plagued his years of service. This same man who'd marched for civil rights in the sixties; supported gay, lesbian, and health care rights in the nineties; and who by 2001 had become one of the senior senate chicken hawks paving the road for the 2003 (semi) coalition invasion of Iraq. A Judas-minted independent, he lacked independent skepticism of Zionism. Bob had studied the strategy and had equally consumed the data decidedly concluding that the Wahabbist train that puttered in the ineptitude of its engines in Saudi Arabia was ultimately fueled and fortified by Waterman and his cronies, with special mention to the modeling offered courtesy of Blackwater and friends. It was their joint contribution that brought the creation and empowerment of "non-state actors" to surge: Al Qaeda in Iraq (ISIS), Al-Nusra Front, Boko Haram, Al-Shabaab, Shabaab al-Islam, Ansar al-Islam, and others. It's a long list and a lot of horror. The list of those to be thanked for it is also long, but Waterman ain't near the bottom of it. By 2016, Waterman was singing the praises of the flim-flamming finger-fucker who won that year's presidential election. For Bob, this raised Waterman on his list of fuck-monkeys he might have to malletize.

As Bob ponders Waterman's jowly face, he comes to terms with the fact that he cannot fully factor out the man's service from his sin. Today, mercy reigns. Bob settles back into thoughts of that crazy nun he'd left behind. He closes his eyes, and just as he begins to reimagine her beside him, he better-yets seeing her squatting on a porcelain loo, pissing un-primped and perfect.

The train comes to a screeching halt.

Eyes flashing open, Bob surveys the situation. Now from nowhere two porters plow past Bob through the train car, rushing into the lead car beyond. They open one door, cross the linkage, and enter the second car, its door closing quickly behind them. Passengers, including Waterman, are animated in their alarm. Bob notes that the train has stopped on a section of track between Baltimore and DC, where looking out of the windows of either side on the train, one can see only field, fence, or chickens. No structures in sight. The sound of sirens on approach and silent cock-a-doodle-dos. Bob lowers his hand to Margaret's purse. Police vehicles abruptly appear, careening through the fields scattering roosters, hens, chicks as they merge toward both sides of the train. Bob opens the zipper to Maggie's farm, stealthily grasps his mallet, but does not remove it from the bag. He waits. Now, over the train's PA system, the conductor's voice. "Sorry, folks, it looks like we're going to be here for a while. We have had to stop the train due to police activity."

Is it a terror attack? Have the bad guys gotten onto Bob? What's all the fuss about?

But after a few tense minutes, the message is passed from the front of the train to the back. Someone has committed suicide by train.

Bob slips his hand out of the purse and rezips the bag. Again, he closes his eyes and imagines Annie's thighs, slowly slipping to sleep.

Sleeping Bob, the Bob who once divorced his slumber from dreams, denying the scheming images and echoes of a lyin' wife long gone. Sleeping Bob, who now lets enter the images of Annie here, there, and gone.

He sees himself in the summer,
a blue bound boy

heading home to a blue bound house.
A blue bound bloodhound
waiting at his door.
A cracked toy of joy
parceled on the kitchen floor
and the late breaking nightly news
on his TV set.
With the news
come the blues.
And as sunset ensues,
Annie exits
his blue bound house.

The images stutter, blur, losing lens on Annie to a scape of blackened ink.

A voice:

"Take the tests, Bob…take the tests."

Bob is confused. "What? Who's there?"

"Just take the Goddamn tests, Bob."

Still only inkscape until static sparks begin to rain within, revealing a figure from the darkness. A skinny, balding man with cyanide eyes and cigarette breath, his movements animated and implanted teeth overly pronounced.

"The tests?" Bob asks.

"JUST TAKE THE GODDAMN TESTS, BOB!!!"

"What tests?" Bob asks. "I don't know what tests you mean."

"THE TESTS. THE TESTS. THE TESTS. TAKE THE GODDAMN TESTS. I'M TRYING TO HELP YOU, MAN!" The skinny man, in the cool of decorative jack-

et-leather, maintains his scrawny body and unpleasant-
ly exaggerated features reminiscent of a stretch'ed elf.
"I'm going to save you, Bob. They want to make me Man
of the Year, Poet Laureate, maybe even the Nobel prize,
and I'm Goddamn well gonna be."

"Do I know you?" Bob inquires.

"Everyone wants you to get the Goddamn tests. Your
mother, your father, Mr. Gerschlaug, Ms. Mayo, your ex-
wife, the president himself—they've all been briefed."

"Briefed?" Bob asks. "By who? By you? Who are you?"

The man breathes down on Bob in vapid violation
of personal dream space. His baldness, bulbous nose,
and bleach-ed porcelain titanium-anchored teeth like an
electrically operated cadaver. "I will lie about you to your
friends, Bob!"

"What friends?"

The man begins to laugh. Bob locks up the taunter's
stick figure and snaps its creepy, crawling frame in half.
With crack of bone and tear of flesh, the pencil piñata of a
person bleeds the confetti of plagiarized pop paeans.

—

BOB IS JOLTED FROM his nightmare when the conductor's
voice announces that another train has arrived and that
all passengers should begin transferring through their
nearest exit. Over transition planks, they transfer train to
train. When the transfer is complete, and Bob has found
another seat, he wonders where Waterman may have
wandered. He'd be on this second train now somewhere.

The doors close and the journey to DC recommences.

Who was that man in his dream, distinctly unlicensed
or invited by any instinctual or intuitive revisitation? Bob
ponders all memory and projection. Dreams already rare,
this one leaves Bob a bit indignant. It must have been
meant to be dreamed by the skinny man himself and
somehow was wrongly delivered to Bob's sleepy head.

As Bob slept, the passengers had come to a consensus,
a conclusion as to the nature of the police action and some
description identifying the victim. Two seats behind Bob's,
a man scribes an email. Bob's ears perk to the tone of every
letter punched. His extraordinary auditory augmentation
of reality systems rarely fails him, and rendering words in
the rear of his retina with their visual vibrations, punch by
punch, letter by letter, Bob's internal cinema displays the
email as it's being written.

D-e-a-r A-m-y,

A-l-l c-l-e-a-r a-n-d o-n o-u-r w-a-y a-g-a-i-n.
T-u-r-n-s o-u-t t-h-e g-u-y w-h-o k-i-l-l-e-d
h-i-m-s-e-l-f w-a-s s-o-m-e 9-0-y-e-a-r-o-l-d m-a-n
i-n a-n e-l-e-c-t-r-i-c w-h-e-e-l-c-h-a-i-r. A-c-c-o-r-d-i-n-g
t-o t-h-e c-o-n-d-u-c-t-o-r, h-e b-u-z-z-e-d o-n-t-o
t-h-e t-r-a-c-k l-a-s-t m-i-n-u-t-e, t-h-r-o-w-i-n-g u-p
t-h-e N-a-z-i s-a-l-u-t-e. C-o-u-l-d-n-'t-'a h-a-p-p-e-n-e-d
t-o a n-i-c-e-r g-u-y. H-a h-a h-a. S-e-e y-o-u
s-o-o-n, h-o-n-e-y (w-i-t-h a b-i-g n-e-w b-o-x o-f
c-i-g-a-r-s).

L-o-v-e,

J-o-b-y

Thirty thousand passengers pass through Union Station every day. A Washington insider, Murray Waterman is an old hand navigating below the vaulted ceilings of its Guastavino tiles and Beaux-Arts architectural tombs. The ease of rolling luggage keeps him in stride, evading attention by critic, fan, or side as he goes it with an invisibility, as inside his head he sings simple songs of a privately imagined Broadway musical, himself at its center.

> *I was once a sitting senator*
> *I had it all back then*
> *power, prestige, and dignity*
> *where did it go and when?*
> *But now it is the season,*
> *of cherry blossom bloom*
> *yet here, post age of reason*
> *rains unseasonal abort blossoms*
> *from womb.*

Murray's inner song interrupted by one now sung aloud. Bob has followed his tracks. Behind Murray stands Margaret proud.

> *Once there was a book of clues,*
> *I guess its critics didn't hear the news.*
> *And while they hoped they'd stop its charge,*
> *it follows right behind you*
> *like a woman looming large.*

Murray stops in his tracks, turns to Bob, who stops in his. "Were you singing that to me?"

"I thought you were singing to me," answers Bob.

Murray's face confesses to finding Margaret fetching. "Do I know you, ma'am? I know I saw you on the train."

"You don't know me, Senator," Bob answers like a girl, "but I know you."

"Let me ask you," murmurs Murray. "Would you like to have some lunch with me?"

Bob has rarely been flirted with by men, but he knows a septuagenarian chubby when he sees one and Murray's crotch is sporting. Bob assumes Murray's fantasy of firkytoodle and forgoes it. "Thank you, but I have an appointment I cannot change."

"Well, maybe we can do it another time?"

"Maybe," says Bob's girl voice. And with a "ta-ta," Margaret is on her way, leaving Murray, alas a burn bag[13] buffoon, sullied but alive.

As Bob exits the station, the roundabout is teeming with taxis, tourists, tricksters, and travelers. A busker covers Phil Ochs.

> *Millionaires and paupers walk the hungry streets*
> *Rich and poor companions of the restless beat*
> *Strangers in a foreign land*
> *Strike a match with trembling hand*
> *Learn too much to ever understand*
> *But nobody's*
> *Buying flowers*
> *From the flower lady.*

---

13   A receptacle for classified documents in which they will be spontaneously destroyed.

STATION EIGHT

CHILDHOOD CHUMS

JOHNNY PAULSON WOULD DIE by drowning at thirteen. Gidget Crainey, she got killed by a kidnapper at fourteen while hitchhiking to the shore. Billy Mix sold and sniffed cocaine and careened off a cliff in his car at nineteen. Willie White shot himself in the stomach after losing a high school fight. Ol' Grist turned out to be a pedophile and went to prison at twenty-two. And that's not to mention Sheldon Sheets and Roger Hornaday. Sheldon decided to run his Range Rover through a crowded crosswalk on a summer afternoon, stripped down to his birthday suit and screamed something about God before being sent to the Camarillo asylum. And Roger topped it all. He made a 911 call, reported himself while raping his own mother, and by the time the cops got there had stabbed her about forty times. These were the boys and girls Bob knew best in grammar school.

The weirdness of the white-skinned and pale-blue-collared communities in our country had already taken solid root by the time of Bob's birth, though it would be decades before these deviances were seen in a more blinding light. In the sixties and seventies, when otherwise decent boys from decent families were delighting in indecency, they did so without knowledge of their own parents' far more impoverished proclivities. Drug-induced orgies and homemaker-curated bordellos were the sort of thing Bob had a nose for at an early age. His own parents were cut from a cloth more conventional, keeping their blinders on if only with a little booze. Bob would never seek to bust their bubble at the dinner hour with his acute observations as to the absurdity stewing in their shared suburbia. This is where one may find the modeling and ultimate makeup of the man. First, there would have been the battle for being believed. "Hey, Ma. Hey, Pop. Guess what the Pattersons are doing…?" Bob imagined the payoff of such a proclamation would have been punishment, his pop packing Pond's soap in Bob's mouth. With that, Bob convinced himself that lewd truisms were generally better left unsaid.

Between the conventions of the home his parents made and the parental pitfalls plaguing so many of his playmates, Bob's foundational understanding of those codes of considered privacy found conflict with those of sinful secrecy. Like any boy in search of direction and the wisdom to weave his way between such worries, he'd have to blast free. This is how bombs came to bloom beyond metaphor and give young Bobby so damned much stuff to do. And from that so much would come a single thing. As if all his thoughts, his dreams, his drive, and knowledge were fillers in time for a funnel focused into a laser-guided stream of service.

In 1982, Bob boarded a plane to Belfast. He was in his early twenties and having heard about the Troubles, he thought in some way he might find some small role in their resolution. He landed in London and made the connection. He had a right-side window seat in economy, and on approach he could see the Northern Irish port city through a light rain in gray. Buildings like a sea of industry, patina-domed churches and sites of institution. As the plane descended to five hundred or so feet above ground, a clock tower approximately a quarter mile off ninety degrees starboard caught Bob's eye and exploded. Typically, the bombings Bob had been aware of took place at ground level, so there was something scintillating about being welcomed to the city by a blast at eye level. Sadly though, for Bob, the plane's engines muted the bomb's report, as lamentably the distance from the tower absorbed the energy wave of its concussion.

Once off the plane and making his way through the airport, he noticed the seemingly casual presence of soldiers pacing with long-barrel automatic weapons and knew he wasn't in the San Joaquin Valley anymore. He went through customs calmly and stepped out in front of the airport, waving a cab. Bob introduced himself to the driver, who disappointingly was a Dave and not a Paddy.

Dave had some kind of lilt in his voice, but definitely not Irish. Bob had seen enough Lucky Charms commercials to know what Irish should sound like, and it definitely was not Dave. He made no plans for shelter in advance and asked fake-Irish Dave for suggested quarters. Dave first described the Europa Hotel in the center of town but cautioned that it had a bit of a *compound* feel to it. It was protected by blast walls, barbed wire, and magnetometers. Every guest or visitor going in or out was subject to search. When Bob told Dave a more open place would appeal to him, Dave took him to the edge of town, where the countryside bled into the city's streets. There, Bob checked into a little bed-and-breakfast joint with the unmemorable name: Bed and Breakfast. In the entry room, it would be the first time he fell in love at nearly first sight with a fat girl. She stood behind a small, unstocked bar that served as a front desk. Fat, rosy-cheeked, and red-haired…finally, real Irish. But as he went to speak to her, her welcome arrived with yet another Dave-like delivery of diction.

"Are there any actual Irish here?" Bob asked.

"Everone here is Irish."

"I'm not. I'm not Irish."

"Fair'nuff, and clearly not, but the rest of us, we most certainly are."

Bob offered her a skeptical glare. "I don't know," he said. "You don't sound Irish to me."

"Ah," said the girl, "And you sound to me like an American who's seen too many Lucky Charms commercials." She continues, but now with a put-on Irish accent of cliché. "Wouldja like a room, wouldja?"

"Now you're talkin'," Bob said. "I got shot once."

"Didja?"

"Yes, I did."

"Seems you'd like to tell me about it. Are ya tink'n gittin' shot an Irish ting? You're lookin' now for good favor."

"Why were you disguising your accent when I first walked in?"

The girl reverts back to her natural Northern Irish. "Probably your cabbie did the same."

"As matter of fact, he did."

"Right," she says, handing him a room key. "Six pounds twenty per night. You pay by the day."

"Can you take American dollars?"

"I can take 'em if they're not counterfeit."

"I'm not a criminal."

"So you say."

Bob presents US dollars in overpayment. The girl pockets it without giving change. "Breakfast starts at seven, ends at nine. There's a pub on Lily Street, two blocks left of the building. You're in room three, right above, top'a the stairs."

Bob is determined to tell his story of having been shot. "Twenty-two caliber long rifle, senior year of high school."

"Fascinatin'," she says. "Just there at the top of the stairs. Enjoy your stay."

But Bob was beginning to be pulled in by her plump and red hair. "I never got along so well with Billy Mix.

But when I was fifteen, a few of us drove out to the Mojave Desert to shoot his rifle and ride motorcycles. And mostly to drink beer."

"Lovely," says the girl. "Motorbikes, guns, and beer—very American of you boys. I suppose we're having a chat now, are we? You're not bad lookin', but you're a bit of a strange man, aren't ya? Should I be throwin' ya out the door?"

"He said it was an accident. I was resetting the cans."

"Resettin' the cans, were ya?"

"I was resetting the cans and all of a sudden my entire skeleton vibrated. The next thing I know, I hear a kind of popping sound—that was the gunshot. The sound comes second."

"Gotcha right in the cock, did he?"

"Excuse me?" Bob inquires.

"Your man," she says. "Right in the cock. Shotcha right in the cock."

"No," Bob explains. "In the shin."

"The shin was it?" she asks. "Your cock runs short'a ya shin and you're expecting me to take some interest in ya, are ya?"

"Yes, my penis does settle well above my shin."

The girl moves from behind the bar to the front door. She locks it and turns a tethered sign toward the front. The sign once read BACK IN A HALF HOUR but has been modified by crossing out the A HALF, replacing it with a FIVE, and adding an s to the end of the HOUR.

She relieves Bob of his ruck, carrying it for him as she leads him up the stairs to room three. "Well let's go take a look at all that, shall we?"

~ ROOM THREE ~

Freckles, flab, and bodacious breasts
bounce young Bob Honey all over his bed.
Hair in his face,
all of it red.
Whiskey and cigarettes
in the breath of all she said.
Bob was ecstatic
and when it was over,
nearly dead.
For five straight days the routine repeated.
He'd wander Belfast streets
when at the bar she was needed.
The struggles, the Troubles,
so thick in the air,
yet Bob went unnoticed
by all who were there.
At the headquarters of the RUC,
he yelled to a guard in black mask,
he called to the tower,
"Hey! Can you see me?"
Then some boys in a Fiat
drove by at high speed,
threw a petrol bomb out the window,
screaming, "Up with Sinn Féin!"

Black burning fuel,
Bob's favorite smell.
He breathed it deeply
to share the children's hell.
The terror of bouncing bullets,
raids and bomb blast
for those who have heard them
sounds and anguish ever last.

Back at the BnB
he found the front door locked.
The sign in the window:
"Back in five hours,
I'm being cocked."

STATION NINE

...AND THE FALL THROUGH THE AIR OF THE TRUE[14]

B EYOND THE TRAIN STATION's roundabout, Bob boards
a bus bound for Sixteenth Street. Pressing play on his
stereophonic synapses, "Gabriel's Oboe" fires in an internal
victual of volume. His mind, as if on autopilot, begins rumi-
nating reconnaissance. The District of Columbia is widely
known to stand above a cheese of subterranean Swiss. The
sub-surfacing of high-voltage overhead feeders, intercon-
necting tunnels, power lines, transformers, switches, and
circuits—some as new as next week, others a fractured infrastructure of nineteenth-century drainage systems. Dupont
Circle alone stands above catacombs worthy of explora-
tion. The former station of streetcar systems, later bus lines,
and briefly a fallout shelter that became an ill-fated food

---

14   "Ralph wept for the end of innocence, the darkness of
man's heart, **and the fall through the air of the true**, wise friend
called Piggy." —William Golding, *Lord of the Flies*

court, now finds favor in the arts.[15] With the expansion of
the greater DC area came added levels of deluge with rains.
Pollutants and runoff had worked off a combined sanitary
system for years, but the additional water and waste led to
extreme CSO.[16] Catching up with the modern age meant
moving away from massive underground storage tanks
and other gray infrastructures, to go beyond *storing and
settling*[17] to green projects of actual infiltration. Bio-reten-
tion filter-strips along streets and sidewalks are a sure sign
of system upgrades. Directional boring bore spacers, cable
racks, and ducts in active Pepco projects. With the Potomac watershed and the Chesapeake Bay at high risk, Pepco
along with the District of Columbia Waterworks have been
taking on billions in projected costs for improvements.
Combine this with the network of tunnels accessing White
House, Pentagon, and Capital for emergency extractions of
politicians and political staffs, and you got yourself a maze
only a master could make out. Add the tunneled train systems, both public and private, and now you have a doozy of
underground structural dissection in this district. Finally,
and perhaps most significantly, below-surface high-meth-
ane storage in MOFs[18] with acrylate links. Representing
the volumetric capacity of crystal structures and methane

---

15   The Dupont underground is now home to a subterranean
arts and cultural organization.

16   Combined Sewer Overflow.

17   Binary water storage system using floating valves to trig-
ger syphoning from one tank to another for storage.

18   Metallic Organic Frameworks

absorption properties in frameworks of ZINC! But Bob's
robust capacity for reverse engineering along with his duti-
fully surgical sensibilities were certain to avail him of a sci-
entific sortie of systems simplified in a synergism in this city
ranked third in energy efficiency and from Plato to Pythag-
oras a post-trivium quadrivium will intersect mathematics,
fractal theorem, philosophy, astronomy, and music through
the libation of liberal arts (more on that anon).

Bob figures he'll go big, deboarding the bus outside the
Hay-Adams Hotel. This upscale Italian Renaissance palace
boasts views of blooms and the White House too. *Margaret*
drags his way to the bar. There before him, as if made from a
dream, sit two fat flamfoo figurines of the derby-hat brigade,
both erring on the side of elderly. He pulls up a barstool in
proximity to the pair. The women exchange *"Oh my goodness!"* retorts to the other's flabbergasted rhetoric. It seems
to Bob they've likely spent many hours slurping pumpkin
old-fashioneds and gabbing in the culture of complaint
by the steady streaming fuel of family disturbance.[19] One
wobbles to stand, excusing her heft to the ladies' room as
the other makes unsubtle excuse, "Darling, I've got to get to
that flight or Morty will be terribly upset. It's been so lovely
to see you again. I know you like your time alone, but if you
get lonely here in the next week you know you can call me."
They tub-to-tub hug goodbye, with the first moving toward
the ladies' room as the other exits the bar.

Inside a lady's stall, Margaret's mark winces as her
whiskey-wee parts the wings of her wizard's sleeve-thing

---

19   Slang for whiskey.

with a sting, until the mercy of Margaret's mallet gives her head a ring. Locked behind him, the stall door gives Bob time to work after sliding out from under it on his back. He makes his way to the hotel laundry, finds a maid's uniform that he makes his own. Now pushing a laundry bin, he returns as maid Margaret to the stall. He breaks through the latch with a swift kick, does a fireman's lift of the lady's heft, and promptly drops her in the bin. He reaches into her purse, taking identification and room key, before covering her with the linen flap and wheeling her out a side door.

There, beside the hotel, a manhole cover. He pulls the mallet from Margaret's purse, prying the manhole cover open with the handle. He dumps the body into the manhole, but it doesn't seem to be an easy fit. He stands above his victim, her body wedged half in and half out of the public street. He studies the dilemma. Now, backing off a few steps from the plugged hole, and then a few steps more. He takes a semi-starting position and jolts forward, vaulting the body. From midair, he kicks down, punching one foot into the small of her broad back, dislodging the body, plunging it into the hole. It nosedives into the methane-filled pit below.

BINGO! Splash.

No harm, no foul. Manhole cover replaced.

It's going to be a beautiful, bountiful day for Bob.

Bob enters the room of the departed, moving to its eighth-floor window. There, across the vista of the north lawn in the late day's sun, the White House. Now sitting at an Italian desk, he writes:

Dear Mr. Landlord,

Remember me? Bob, Bob Honey. Like you, I am planning a little surprise for October. Whoopsy! It is October, isn't it? It's been on my mind just how much we have in common, you and I. It is true, isn't it? Human processing cannot keep pace with the velocity and volume of the masses' many voices. Their direction diluted to distraction and designed to eliminate the individual human thought. Psychics and wordsmiths may, like you, claim the origination of tracking algorithms in those for whom rectitude has receded. I too have often found it difficult to put my feelings into words, believing that it should not be so much what we say that matters, but how we feel the words as we say them. Similarly, not what others say to us, but how we might believe their words true at the moment they are spoken. You see, with savagery awakened, I could choose to be your defender, make a case for an epoch in which your mind is most sane. I've seen the seven-year-old sleeved in tattoos of dragons and a rendition of the Rifleman on his back while his parents pledged to you in a booth. It has been said that for those who have had to face the premature deaths of their own children, denial is itself a far too recklessly disparaged tool of grace in the machining of necessary quietudes with which we counter disturbingly painful volumes. What would be the implications, however, if only silence could speak truth? If fake is in fashion, please don't talk to me about spring collections, and you can tell your wife that while there is no Quranic legitimacy for burkas, similarly, it is also illegitimate to mannequin-mindedly model attention-getting slogans while feigning sympathy for separated Salvadorians and other

desperate sprouts from down south. Count me as no longer
in a liminal state. I'd believe you a man of truth so long as I'd
stand by lying eyes. So listen, Lassie, I'm letting you know
there's going to be some really big news. Some really, really,
really big news. It's going to be HUGE. No gun or pink mist
like that JFK tryst. Your fake news, my fuck-yous news. I'll
leave you one of my clues—you snooze...etc. Get it? In my
life, I have been mocked, maligned, conned, and exploited in
ways a man of your caricature can never comprehend. I know
with intimacy threats most extreme, and the ways and places
too horrifying to utter or ask of your imagining. I've got a good
sense of your status mobility system, whether stabbings or
intuitive scramble coerced in carnival talk. Upon your passing,
there will be no loving tributes, no partisan myths to make or
keep. No maverick memory, though memory will remember
the creep who crept by day and night in plain sight. All will
only be left with all there'd ever been to know; all of what
you'll have made of children's pain by a man whose ego bled
in vain. I'm sending you my firstborn and six simple words:
Tweet me, bitch. I dare you.

—

BOB SPENDS THE NEXT thirteen hours grieving images on
the hotel tube, flicking from news network to news network, governing the gossamer left to hold up the country.
Then come the Humpty Dumptys, the pitchmen and wom-
en once known as thespians until their vainglorious leap
from Wonderland's wall. Sometimes, Bob drifts into a consideration of the goodness of guns. The lethality of a partic-

ular pistol caliber carbine that can be quickly disassembled, concealed, and carried, and the inadvertent promotion of polymer weapons crafted by 3-D printer. But Bob wouldn't be Bob in any return to ballistics. His only option is to focus all his gifts and grace on the labyrinth of an engineering fuse that may in a mighty miracle detonate destiny by force of mallet. This is no time, Bob thinks, to let morality's panic-pathology justify his aversion to technology. Hostile takeovers must be taken on their own terms and turf. If necessary are all means, then by no means would Bob bristle at branding. Boom—he would make the bad guy paranoid of the sky, and the magazine mannequin pursing her lips expose what she hides of high-riding hips, those like a handbag overstuffed with narcissistic sex toys, then show that her shoulders give her away, so thick when she's at rest.

—

HE'D LEFT HIS LANDLORD's letter to lay there on the Italian desk. Returning, he brushes the letter aside and pulls a bit more hotel stationery from the drawer. Placing it before him, he briefly clocks the marble base of a desktop lamp and suffers the tiniest of temptations to let Annie's form emerge from it in delicate dance. In resistance, he returns to the stationery, making maps and marking them in a braced momentum. He considers magnets, mole dives, and skip charges. The symphonic structure of his strategy continues in refinement for twenty-odd sleepless hours. He orders more stationery from the concierge. It is delivered and delved into. By 8:00 p.m. the next day, he wakes from a brief sleep surrounded by the physics, ballistics, mathematics, and madness of the systematically scribed details he's designed with a mind monopolized by manifest destiny. His patriotism ever unyielding to white flags of floccinaucinihilipilification, Bob is back on the block and will continue at pace.

MEMORANDUM

FROM: The Office of the Deputy Director of ████████
CLASSIFICATION: HIGHLY CLASSIFIED
DISTRIBUTION DATE: ████████

This memo is not for distribution and intended for use by members of the ████████ and designated ████████ USG officials only.

SUBJECT: Project Rogue
THREAT LEVEL: HIGH
MEANS OF RECOVERY: Triggered autonomous internal hotlist cyber monitors. Intercepted prior to distribution.

> To: Mr. Robert Honey
> RE: My Appetite for Rats
> Sender: ████████████████

Mr. Honey—

I've changed my mind with regards to entering portions of your body into a Cuisinart. I now favor the notion of force-feeding you a fragmentation grenade on a football field. It is my thought to recruit a team of interns (say 12–15 young people) and equip them with jam jars and putty knives. I'll ask them to scrape what remains of you from the grass of the gridiron and transfer those scrapings, like the paste of your remains, into the jars. Invariably, each jar will also collect the blades of grass and refuse I call roughage.

How's life on the run? I've always had my own thoughts and fantasies of running away from it all. Blending in with the masses. Seems such a freeing scheme. So I'm just so curious, how free does it feel? Do you find it hard to keep fit? Me, I like to eat good food and work out at Equinox. You probably wouldn't approve. This behavior, this preference would be antithetical to such a puritan of antisocial pathos…

Sorry, I fell asleep there for a moment.

Sincerely,

████████████████

ANALYSIS and RECOMMENDATION: Unchanged
This pattern of misses now seems at the moment an exercise in the agent's private venting. As with previous memo dated ██████████, current input was written but unsent, and similarly without evidence that Agent ██████–057 is currently in possession or has any current knowledge of SUBJECT ROGUE whereabouts. Agency should continue monitoring.

PART TWO

"The thing is—fear can't hurt you any more than a dream."

—William Golding, *Lord of the Flies*

STATION TEN

PUZZLE PEACE

WHAT HAD BROUGHT HIM here? As if sitting on the black bank of the Rubicon, his boat burning plank by plank like a martyr to *Marie-Celeste*.[20] There had been Bukowski's beautiful suggestion that "sometimes you get so alone it just makes sense." But for Bob, in this his most solitary and severe of seasons, it had led him to a wholly heightened sense of citizenship in solidarity and opened to the only gang we ever get—the good and bad, the evil and sad, the cowards, the crumbs—but like 'em or not, they're the only history we've got. He began to see their spirit faces as if being carved from the flaming planks of his burning boat. Former foes surrounding in support. Castaways from his many muddied lives. Even ex-wives began to dull their knives by his side. One by one the river

---

20   In 1872, an American cargo ship, the *Marie-Celeste*, was found in the North Atlantic adrift and in perfect condition. It remains a mystery what became of its crew.

delivered all those who had been adrift in memory, now
seemingly saved, from current to riverbank in deliverance
to Bob Honey, humble enough to just do stuff. There was
the cowboy and teenage black chick. Mom, Dad, and
a gaggle of Stingray riding runts who'd written REDRUM
on a Nazi neighbor's wall. There were blow-dart-blowing
Guineans, Spurley, and a spear-gun-wielding orthodox
Jew. A lesbo-leaning liberal and Pappy Pariah too. Bloated
bodies of a southern storm finally facing upward as if
deistic flotillas offered to lift Bob's force. The Helen Mayos
one and two. These faces, places, and the bombworks of
boy-Bob, all adversities born again by blades of flame,
cutting carvings from seaworthy wooden grain. Through
all the pillage, pathos, poverty, and pain, these faces
unrefrained, uncontained, and now looming unfurled in
all the grotesque that is this most beautiful world, where
love, if not the outreach of damage, has no reach at all
until the spellbound silence of a Parkland girl's call.

—

BOB'S TEMPTATION TO MOVE toward euphoric reattach-
ment, a calculated caution to be most carefully considered.
He'd been born to see a generation of optimism drowned
by neo-liberalism, long hair, and needles drooping from
punctured veins. He'd seen California Quaker and Har-
vard kraut murder twenty thousand additional American
boys in the treasonous power play of a political campaign
(Oh, Henry!). These significant signs of his time and his
own travels through acid storms had shown him only the

gangrenous dormant derma of human disposition. And those few aspiring angels who had listed LSD their license to soar—in surrendering to chemical conceits, had they leapt from tall buildings in a dream to fly, they instead die. Armed with this cache of reservation, Bob reverts to the backup systems of skillsets set to satisfy the justifications of antisocial behaviors. Critical field operators are often accused of subjectivism. Bob perceives this as scrutiny by a sissy society, and with rectitude, his situational awareness would part terrestrial penumbra to prevail. He'd breathe in, then out. Hold breath, repeat. In resolve, he opted to believe. He'd give the gang another go. Their faces, now finally cut to discernibility by the fire they'd sewn, display themselves to Bob as charred and buzzing forms for the purpose they were born. These who in their core were born as horseflies fit for war.

"Are you going to war, my Bob-beam?"

—

THERE IT IS, THAT voice in its whispered tone. That voice he'd so long known. The one that when gone altered his world's atmosphere, hosting a new variant of air absent the sweetness of her breath. His brain now beckons it back. *Hers*, never blackened by a fire's charring fury, remained with Bob, the wings of an angel defying a virulent sky. Not like his cadre of sureños in body and buzz of blue tail fly.

"Annie, is that you? You don't have to tell me. You don't have to say a word. I know your sound and feel your hum. War is no longer war when no decency minds the store.

Bob is going to a better kind of battle. I don't know if Bob is me. There is an old man who often watches. Sometimes he's black, sometimes he's white, and I think he's from Kentucky. I think I've begun to use his words. Words I'm told are worth study. Without you this man feels closer and closer. I want to feel you close enough to kill him, to make him go away, but darling I cannot see if this man just might be me."

"Oh my Bob-beam, let it be just a bad dream. Let my voice and heart be real. Your Annie is as close as you choose to feel."

There is, it seems to Bob, a kickoff point. A certain something in the articles of man's nature so that he might elicit most from love or ire. Bob's had happened with the advent of one hot bullet to his brain in a posh Miami suite surrounded by the skylight shards of glistening mallet-mangled glass and a sheet-swathed prostitute screaming for her passport. In what might to some bode badly for Bob's battles, Bob sensed himself headed to a prescient place. A place less alone. The laws had all been broken, baring them as the silly cinematic sensibilities of babies. But damn the babies. Only leaders love. A time comes when one's gotta own up to nature, and its most direct drive nourished match and mate on demand. On one hand, Bob had a plan. On the other, he was ready to imagine that beyond a plan, beyond the gang of gangsters summoned of an anguished past, would come a pleasure. A person. A partner. One who, like Bob, would be ready and willing to pull the plug on propriety, take a peek at the puzzle, and put themself in whatever well-appointed place invited their piece. Until those who *can* begin to *do*, the puzzle is paused in paralysis. And for Bob, so long impregnated with pause, it would be uncanny if that partner—that *person*—were finally Annie. That one whose smile, like heaven's shield, he trusted would keep her safe, warm, and wild.

—

HERE NOW ON RUBICON's bank would Bob break earth. Digging deeply into its moistened soil for organic anthrax, slathering its muddy toxins over his body as shield to the charlatans, shylocks, and sheep of his quarry. A swamp beast branded, and Willernick[21] born.

> *BRANDING IS BEING!*
>
> *Yes! This is the it of it, and so be it.*
> *Bob becomes a Willernick.*
> *Now, a Willernick is a vastly wilder thing than any half-man/half-beast,*
> *or even, and by a long shot, any former Nazi in loud electric hunting chair*
> *chasing child over honeysuckle hedge.*
> *So, now would Bob finally become his brand.*
> *Set a date with Mr. Real Estate.*
> *Whoops,*
> *the wide-eyed smoking boy, flash-framed once more through fissure,*

---

21 A post-Jurassic terra-aquatic hybrid beast with hooves.

he asks as if in the familiar,
"What's up, Mr. America?"
Here's what's up, thinks Bob:
No more nerves nor apologies for pocket protectors
or perseverance.
No sir, ladies and gentlemen.
No ma'am, ma or pa.
"I'm from California," Bob thought.
A boy born of the SJV.
Former resident of Woodview with a warrior's
word to the wise.
Earthquakes come in all shape, shift, and size.
Free to fondle the lithosphere.
Find a plot of land at fault,
open its wound,
and flood it with salt.
No mortgage, no escrow.
Energy shifts of tectonic plate
will I move to manipulate.
For this country, so rich in poverty,
I will buy it,
I will buy it,
a Honey
of a property.

So this was Bob's intumescent reaction of heart and mind. Risings not *from* but *of* ash. Character in commonality to freaky Pharaoh's serpents[22] seething within his

---

22   A chemical reaction of sodium bicarbonates forming snakelike forms of burning ash.

senses. And what else could be expected of pop psychology seducing society's money-in-hand herd to shrink from responsibility? Truth itself, now a Holy Grail to human nature's indulgence and propensity to the flagrant flexibility of facts. Give every man, woman, and child their *own* truth so that there may be none to go around. Within the cleaved fraction of a moment, disguising itself in indecision's mask while tempting ideals to escape, like leaked water droplets ding-tinging on a hot plate, short and court electrical fire.

In an effort to transcend doubt, Bob would serve the preconscious of his birth canal consciousness clawing for survival. In Bob's *born* assumption, melee is man's most morbid inheritance and marginally taxed morality. Beholden only to the nuance of black and white being right until it's wrong.

There is no nuance in the now-world of nuclear proliferation. Bob would take only the smart lessons from that dumb show. On page 43, section 4.2 of the *U.S. Armed Forces Nuclear, Biological, and Chemical Survival Manual* is a hypothesis for the detection of a nuclear or radiological attack:

> Nuclear attack will probably come without warning. There will be a bright flash, enormous explosion, high winds, and a mushroom-shaped cloud indicating a nuclear attack from a true fission or fusion weapon. The first indication will be very intense light. Heat and initial radiation come with the light, and blast follows within seconds. If terrorists acquired and detonated a nuclear device, the attack would likely come

without warning, and therefore initial reactions must be
automatic and instinctive.

It is this measure of initial reactions both "automatic
and instinctive" that seem to Bob most relevant to
revolution. Mining the acknowledged missteps of Che
Guevara's compromised actions in Congo would appear
a most reasonable reflection, but...it at once gave Bob a
headache and as well would take too long. Such would be
Bob's song. Only advertising could threaten the clarity of
human boundaries or buildings, where former craftsmen
and women succumb to selling cars, cosmetics, watches,
fashion, and perfume while technicians fuse their forms
to fictions so farfetched and anti-human in a march to
embody machines. Machines that devalue the currency
of communication and drive the disenfranchised to this
discombobulated wall of words. The horrible humming
of humanity most horrific taking itself hostage by suicidal
selfie stick. Declassifying every part of one's soul in
voluntary distribution of self to Phineas Priests, design
labs, and the man with a parched vagina in the middle of
his face. Humankind's increasing embrace or blindness to
its own festering hypocrisy. If the scrutinizers scrutinized,
they'd be so forever fuckin' screwed. So it is only natural
that there would be, in the air, heirs to legends. Modern
Monkey Wrenchers building bombs for barriers, be they
erected with the pesos or pennies of political posture.
While worries about domestic terror rightly rise, few can
face the hyper-emergence of sophisticated criminality
burgeoning in the American mind. You have friends and

neighbors who are learning both old and new ways to exploit, extort, and rob from the modern man and woman's honest well. Bling rings, butchers, and hackers. You know them. You text them back and forth twice or more a week. A deepening sickness of spirit is extending arms into your ass and pocket. These are facts. It is also a fact that mass killers of Jews from the Romanian Iron Guard installed themselves into the hierarchy of the Catholic Church in America. Why, Bob wonders, is buckshot most often composed of recycled car batteries? He gives that one a good think while listening to the whimsical whistling of his own rendition from the distant empty train car bounding the rails of his temporal lobes, and the world unknowingly begins to sing along with his whistled song...

> *Jim crack corn and I don't care,*
> *Jim crack corn and I don't care,*
> *Jim crack corn and I don't care,*
> *Ole Massa gone away.*

STATION ELEVEN

IT'S A FUCKING BUILDING

I T IS BOB'S AIM to procure the eighteen-acre Pennsylvania Avenue parcel of Secret Service–protected
Potomac-adjacent property. This would be a procurement
fraught with perils. But as it has become a house of def-
amation, so it is a relic symbolic of a nation in need of
amputation. Its gangrenous paw crying out to Bob's bone
saw. Under United States code, title 18, section 871, no one
may willfully make "any threat to take the life of, to kidnap,
or to inflict bodily harm upon the President of the United States." But once upon a POTUS had been the prolific
duties to culture, constitution, and the countenance of a
country. Bob would make no threat, nor do damage of inevitable collateral accountability. He would, however, con-
trive to commandeer coveted turf in service to his country.

Among shelters from shit are beautiful things that
can never be broken. Human things, you know. Human
creations of endless care and courage incorruptible. Paint-

ings, poetry, and the defining music of a generation. In times of trouble, Bob could quiet his mind with memories of this music, meditation, and ever-emerging emergency responses from Madagascar to Mississippi. But when holding onto history threatens tomorrow, it's time that the "clear eye and the kindly heart" of Saroyan's sensibilities be employed in full, and "if the time comes in the time of your life to kill, kill and have no regret." Because also among shelters from shit are the once grand shelters reduced by a redundancy of rape. Those that have come to symbolize fantasies of *fedifrago* females, the Black community, the Brown, LGBTQ, Evangelical-Homophobic-New Testament sodomites, the vegans, the veggies, the lefties, the righties, Chinese, Japanese, boneies, the what-are-these! Not communities, Goddamn it! These are not Goddamn communities outside the omnipresence of pervasive popular perils particular to these populations. Only when it seems that the sky may be falling on us all at once does a community find its calling. That's when it's suddenly most convenient to court a girl, be she pretty or plain, and to discover in savagery a kindness most sustained.

—

DEBATE AS ONE MIGHT the virtues of Bob's prior profession, or even his penchant for purging particular populations, he cannot be undermined nor can he be credibly cursed by the uninventive. Observing the property from his hotel-hide, there are on this day a group of all-male all-white protestors. Making actionable his audacious au-

ditory acumen, Bob raises the window ajar. An Alabama activist with a bullhorn stands at the speaker's podium in opposition to engines of hashtag cultural zealotry. "Reason is in ruin! It's time that we the men of #MeThree behave equally unreasonably in response." A cheer from his sultans of pendulum swing. "We have identified the leadership! All their fathers, brothers, boyfriends, husbands, and sons are now being investigated by our *movement*. These family members' names will be published with requests for any and all information of their treatment of women, men, boys, girls, or ducks over these past thirty years. And as for the women of this leadership themselves, we intend to expose any illicit affairs they've had or have ongoing with the husbands, boyfriends, or girlfriends of their sisters in the cause. Hypocrisy demands its light." Applause from the Caucasian choir of common sense and a ubiquitously institutionalized aversion to art.

Bob, suddenly sullen, closes the window, moves to the edge of the bed, picks up the remote, and turns on the news. The queen of the collusion klutzes' clan of crafty coms coordinators drags the cumbersome bovine body of her anguished and despising spirit to the podium. Cameras click and flash. Journalists joust for her attention. The day's sensation: immigration. All the sanctioned child abuse and its justification. "You're a mother," barks one journalist. "How would you feel if it were your kids separated from you!?"

The hefty oxygen thief answers with accusation. "Did you know that I was asked to leave a restaurant

before my first glass of wine. And why? Because I work for
a president who enforces the law! So unfair!"

Bob flips the channel to a competing station. They say
the president's lawyer is going to flip. A campaign chief of
Atwater arrogance marches into arrest and an Uncle Tom
preacher bends the bible for the king. When a former
CIA chief tweets an administration's commonality with
Nazi causes as a caution, it causes a commotion of denial.
Prepubescent Proud Boys scrawl tough-guy tattoos on
rolls of fast-food-fed blubber. Bob sits sanguine in the
rediscovered sanctuary of his senses when a stalwart
blonde republican pundit begins spewing her seasoned
cyanide through bent and bitter lips.

Wernher von Braun's former fellows from Frankfurt
fudged a few documents placed in a paperclip to get
them to Pharos. Bob flips the television off. He feels
a slight buildup of sweat above his brow—a yearning,
churning call to action. He moves to the minibar, feeds
ice into a glass from a stainless-steel chalice. From the
refrigerator he pulls a bottle of chilled water, pours it
slowly over the ice and into the glass that sits on the
counter above the fridge. Almost immediately the
temperature control of the room conflicts with the
chill of the water in the glass, and condensation drips
from the glass exterior, creating a circle of water on
the countertop. Condensation has always presented
problematic pressures to Bob's biorhythmic dreams of
order, the constant demand to wipe away water rings
from tabletops so seemingly senseless.

He calls the front desk, extending his stay in countdown to caper, continuing to cop the concord of a woman whose body had been interred to cloaca. First, he needs the vital materials to create a mallet of concentrated capacity and minimal weapons signature.

—

From the pantheon of Bob's past lives' portfolio, he recalls a late-nineties government study inspiring the intricacy of his plan. The study's essential notion was to think about what mixes of plant-like robots (burrs, lures, creeper vines) and animal-like robots might be applied to surveillance or applied sabotage. What entrance they might make into secure underground facilities. The imaginings of robotic creeper vines (small robots trailing wires) going down an air duct or up a sewer pipe; or of inducing a person to collect an object—perhaps money— that is actually a sensor (a lure); or of something that attaches to a vehicle that enters the facility (a burr). The advantage of creepers is that the wire provides power and communications (e.g., down a sewer pipe that a radio would not penetrate). Robot navigation has come a long way since the nineties through SLAM (Simultaneous Location and Mapping). Imaging much improved, processors evolved, and elements of robotics far less costly in the advent of said sciences clamor. Solar chip components now allow unit migration to closest available sun for recharge, and then return to operational location. The notion of creating a chain reaction through available technology triggered by mallet began Bob's breakthrough, exploring the vulnerabilities in vibration-powered generators, where in transducers, piezoelectric diaphragms may be disturbed by sound pressure waves. Conversion of kinetic energy from vibration to electrical energy. Resonators amplifying vibration to transducers then remolding their kick from vibricity to electricity. Charge, current, fields, capacitors, resistors and inductors, EM wave propagation, and antenna principals will conspire to capture cables of copper wire where, in conjunction with magnets, their magic might make metals move. This of course will require conscientiously considered placement, and if Bob is anything, he is magnetically conscientious.

STATION TWELVE

THE MATING OF WILD WASPS

ONE MORNING, ANAPHYLACTIC SHOCK shook Sheldon Sheets into seizure in the schoolhouse. Stung as he was by a wasp, he'd recovered exponentially with epinephrine, enough to bully ten-year-old Bob by recess of the same day with a bop to Bob's head. What you see is what you get until you get it, and Bob had thought he'd had it pretty well got…but as it turned out, he sometimes, with some things, did not. Even good character is as unpredictable as its greatest humiliation. The *who* was *who*, and the *what* and *why* of what they do. Sheets had seemed such a sensible, smart, and all-around nice kid, not prone to bullying, though he was big. Bob had not seen it coming, but quickly learned that no character comes completely unflawed, nor impenetrable. Twelve-year-old Sheldon had been baited into this otherwise alien and unprovoked attack on Bob by even bigger boys after being caught crying in reaction to the sting.

Bob had often been the cherry breaker for these fraternal fistfights of face-saving for virgins to violence. For one thing, Bob was scrappy enough that nobody could accuse his fledgling adversary of picking a punk easily prevailed upon. But Bob was also small enough that even the unindoctrinated pugilist might at first feel they had a chance to get out of the fight with a win, or in the worst case without too much damage in their own direction. Win or lose, Bob never had any real aversion to hand-to-hand combat, no fear of physical pain or foe, nor did he find his victories invigorating. If somebody wanted to fight, he'd fight with all his might n'forget the folly before the next day's duty. It was sort of like Sundays, they come and they go.

What was unusual was the Sunday following the fisticuffs with Sheldon. It had gotten around school that Sheldon had a winning right hand, a hand that had taken scrappy Bob off the balls of his feet, landing him hard and heavy where the schoolyard met the street. Rebecca "Jelly Juice" Johnson had earned her nickname, but that's as much as Bob was ever told about it by those who talked too much for his taste. Rebecca had a pretty face under all those freckles and freakishly pale skin but didn't promote it much. Her personality projected as much possibility and potential as one might expect from any partially pubescent public schoolgirl, but defining characteristics had not yet come to fruition, hence few knew her by any name but Jelly Juice. For this and other reasons there had been no recognized indicators in Rebecca's behavior that could have prepared Bob, nor those more in the know, for the retribution she would seek upon Sheldon on the Sunday following the schoolyard scrappery, nor that she would do it, as she solely did, on Bob's behalf (more on that anon).

In the category of odd days on earth, Bob recalls six or seven episodes from his youth where he'd clearly wondered, "Where have all the women gone?" EXAMPLE: It's 3:00 p.m. on a Wednesday in '68. Bob is eight years old, replacing the inner tube of his bicycle's tire. The tire had gone flat beside a busy boulevard of shops. Once wrapped around the rim, he begins to pump the tube while scanning his surroundings, and in that scanning, he notices scant women and girls. The passing cars, drivers and passengers both: only men. The shops, shopkeepers, passersby: only boys and men. Where might be the women of the world on Wednesday at 3:00 p.m. PST? After several such experiences, and each one witnessed only by Bob, he resolved that all women and girls slip slyly away to a weekly meeting. A weekly and super-secret meeting, so slyly secreted that dads don't notice their own daughters' disappearances throughout and until theses meetings' adjournments. There can be no note of reappearance where there has been no notice of absence. One more wicked woman trick? Or just boys' bat eyes? Now one might think that a boy of Bob's resolve might panic in paranoia at his living as the seemingly lone male to possess knowledge of the rhythm and beat of an entire gender's intermittent invisibility to society's gaze.

But no.

Despite the understanding that comfort with the conspiracy of women might make him complicit in complacency, Bob came to consider their conspiracy with a compartmentalization of such rare comfort that he'd soon contain his awareness of it to his subconscious.

Not so Sheldon, who surely could never have known the resources available to a girl as nondescript as Rebecca "Jelly Juice" Johnson. Her life already illuminated with the infrastructure, power, and wisdom inhabited by the secret world of women in weekly meetings managed, as if magically, to include the international and total body of their gender. Be they grown woman or infant child, English or other speaking, rich, poor, black, white, Asian, free or imprisoned...ALL attend in the same systemic timeframe unseen by any boy but Bob.

Far too obvious to influence Rebecca's retribution was the way in which wild wasps mate—that double-backed beasting leading the female to hibernation and the male to death by procreation. Besides, she was only designing the slap of Sheldon's hand and not his execution.

> *Sunday was sunny and warm.*
> *When in church*
> *entered Sheldon's form.*
> *He'd never taken time to learn verses,*
> *and at twelve*
> *was still innocent of most curses.*
> *So when it came time to sing them*
> *to call out for almighty God*
> *to bring them*

he read from a Rebecca-placed and reprinted
prayer book,
sang out the one word repeated
as if a holy hook...
"RAPE-RAPE-RAPE!"
he called out in atonement.
Giving both priest and Sheldon
a learning moment.
The priest he did flee
as Sheldon fell to a knee
where he finally did see
the truth of his own history.
And when the news came to Bob by phone,
he may well have learned a lesson of his own.
One that one day
would come in handy
an inevitable asset,
be it miraculous or dandy...
or both.

STATION THIRTEEN

CLEM CASERTA'S PINE NUT EMPORIUM OF THE FEDERAL DISTRICT

BEHOLD CLEM CASERTA. PROPRIETOR of the Pine Nut Furniture Emporium in the small industrial zone of Ivy City in northeast DC. His establishment less emporium than warehouse/workshop where an old man and his tools have toiled for half a century in the wood and metal trade. Most impressive in the landscape of the shop: a welding station capable of burning thirty thousand pounds of wire per year. Bob eyes it in awe. Thirty thousand pounds of wire per year is a tractor trailer full of welds. The proprietor must have at one time or another been in commercial production. Beads burning much hotter and faster than the traditional welding work Bob's own hands have ever handled. On sight, Caserta looks less Italian than his name implies, his sienna skin a litmus misdirection for Texan Hohokam leads Bob to believe he lives in the witness protection program. A rat who's been skating on too many years of free ice. When Bob pops by on this afternoon, he really *pops* by. With one swift blow of Margaret's mallet, Caserta's proprietary interest in this former train yard establishment collapses along with all memory or existence of the long solitary craftsman's sins. Folded on the floor in a pool of cherry syrup blood, Caserta's lifeless body expels de rigueur its seminal fluids. Above him, perusing the bevy of power and hand tools, is the new owner of Bob's Pine Nut Emporium. This place, pleasing. A perfect plunder and bonanza of machinery. Yet and strangely, while well-tooled, the material stock cupboards, open and empty.

—

LEFT ALONE TO A room of tools that would enable the re-forming and forming of woods and metals beat the button, button, belly button of any means of meditation. Bob is in the end a builder, a maker of things, a mower of lawns, and a master in the manufacturing of sandwiches suited to his palate. Bandsaws, drill presses, planers, grinders, torches, tinners, routers, lathes, all with the scent of man-made things. He felt it like a church of purpose over the pedantic, and as such pledged in prayer to press on.

—

BACK IN THE HOTEL business center, Bob busts through the alien web's windows, identifying a local junkyard where he is later able to scavenge a length of ¾ titanium rod. From the wood scrap pile he carefully selects scraps of hardwoods and softwoods from one-inch panels. Returning to the Pine Nut Emporium, he cuts six-inch circular sections from his collected woods on bandsaw, binding them together with deluxe wood glue and squeezing them in a vise, creating a solid seven-inch cylindrical striker. Next, he refines its contour on a lathe, with an eye on aerodynamics and, as always, aesthetics. From the center point of the cylinder, in both directions, he slightly slants and increasingly narrows toward its impact ends. He mounts it on a drill press, boring through its length with a bit selected for its overused history, which tunnels through the wood leaving the bore snug to the introduction of the titanium rod. Now, using a small sledgehammer, he pounds the rod into place, grinding it flush with the impact ends, and sands both flush ends to a sheen. With a one-and-a-half-inch spade bit, he drills the handle-receiver until he feels its leading tip touch the titanium core. He finds a modern ax hanging on a wall beside a fire extinguisher. Cutting away the ax's head with a miter saw, he fashions its fiberglass haft as a modified long-mallet handle, then into the opposite side of the mallet head, he bores again to the internal rod. With a hammer and chisel, he chips away the interior wood within the bore on both sides of the rod, leaving just enough imperfection to enhance the fate of its frictional squeeze and tension. He then takes the fiberglass haft, cutting into it lengthwise from its top, creating a slip gap in its width that will allow it to slide through the cylinder, around the titanium core, and through the bore. He lathers the newly minted inset

of the handle in high-grip adhesive, lines it up, and slams
it into position. With the fit snug, he tests it, putting his
feet on both sides of the mallet head against the floor, and
attempts to pull the haft out as if Excalibur from the stone.

It doesn't budge.

He fine-grinds excess on the mallet head's top flush
to titanium core. Deadly sweet spots as if damascened.
Bob is locked, loaded, and ready for the dance. His offering of arrhythmic expressions of body. Each of those
orchestrated evenings beginning with the promise of his
pressed pants as he pushed one leg then the other into
hope. This new dance would spark fireworks like none
he'd ever felt. All those murders like masturbation in practice for perfect sex, and when he would slam his hammer
this time, it would release a firing charge with the energy
of perfect love.

—

AND THE KID CARNY barked,

"Be you knave or knight...
Come one! Come all!
COME SLAY THE DRAGON!!!"

Young Bob's carnival barking days began by four each
morning. He would dress, scramble some fluffy eggs, and
get on his way to the bus stop. It would be two hours and
two transfers before he arrived at the foothills below the
fair. A compressor breathed the bus doors open, and little
Bob ambled to the dirt road that led to his destination.
There, he'd throw out his thumb and easily catch a random

ride, from either colleague carny cars or the early arriving flower children seeking prime spots at the head of the line.

Bob liked arriving early. He had a young man's intuit for the value of repetition. Swinging his mallet to the base of the dragon, sending the puck screaming to the bell, he fancied himself a Quasimodo figure to the fair, ringing in each new day. Each new day. Each new sameness. A fusion of pathos, purpose, and patriotism.

STATION FOURTEEN

SYMPHONY OF INFAMY

THOSE IN THE ASCENDANCY of this capital city occupy systemic sensibilities like a lattice of overlapping scars. Sets and subsets of synergies that devolved over generations to own the objectionable with a ferocity never before known. Bob would have to become the master of his own rendition. Today's task: the reverse engineering of an electrically charged Rube Goldberg whereby embedded sensors may be bypassed by deviation of voltage times current-square times current times resistance. Energy generation and automation of the speedy express, bridge- and leg-wire alloys, and an ever-keen awareness that the pores exuding oils for fingerprints live on their friction ridges. This, the close-held information intubated into his body by intuition and the ingenuity of a life lived for problem-solving. He walks blocks, boards buses, dropping magnets and treats of frequency-fucking tourmaline like breadcrumbs, cramming the city's arterial grid into his memory banks for a mile, his magic mile track from thunder of mallet to a people's house in such disgrace. After several hours of rigorous reconnaissance and tiny tech-troop deployments, he has found his sermon's mount.

—

AT SUNSET, BOB SITS below a brass cistern on the toilet seat of his Hay-Adams Hotel suite. He stares into the marble wall to recapitulate that obscene corner of conscious calculation where the clarity to kill thrives. In the lines, shines, and layered language of its geological history, the marble makes a male face, painting stone on the reflection of Bob's own. In the execution of homicide, have they shared a certain something? Something not Godly, but closer to cheap? In this succession of graphic flashes, these friendly flashes within all men of mayhem, harkening from their maiden acts of human dispatch. It comes to him from the rock, the stabbing threat to his inherent aspiration toward moral legacy, a dirty filthy sense of self from a mandatory secret in a life lived striving for some semblance of truth between the sludge and the antiseptic, those increasingly binary norms of a formally civil society. Beneath the reflection's head, the slab shine of stone extends in offering to the decaying hands of his own humanity. He takes them in his and weeps. Though he is not the bigoted bomber of boring bravado waving Confederate flag, not the public personality as human Instagramic billboard, and also not Twitter-bent on the cannibalization of colleagues, nor the shooter of Jews or Blacks in prayer, nor the Saudi scion of a filial dynastic moral dearth, he is in the end a man choosing to cause destruction in a purposeful purge that cannot be empirically certain to secure its purpose soundly. He dreams of ballast stones, their weight in offset of cargo, which when brought to port are unloaded and laid as pavers repurposed for permanent streets. Bob seeks to be a ballast stone, weighing down a load in rubble only to be reborn as road.

"Button, button, bellybutton," Bob breathes. He moves to the desk where his unset missive to Massa lies before him. He folds it with precision, producing a perfect paper Concord. He turns his chair to the White House–facing window, opened in slight gap from its sill. He cocks the Concord and sends it so, barely breaching the gap as if a whisper through a missing tooth. The paper plane's flight perfect to behold, as if touched by the Trinity's tailwind, it traces through the October air over cherry blossoms, gates, and lawn, until its touchdown on tarmac slides it into the hangar of the house's north portico, where it is retrieved by a savvy Secret Service agent.

Well into the evening, an abhorrent acolyte ricochets rumors off satellites rhapsodically. The hyperthyroid darting and descendance of his eyes spell LIES LIES LIES. A regular on the twenty-four-hour menstrual cycle we've become inured to and call news, this one-time New York mayor and lawyer of merit has managed to morph into a Maxipad, as he absorbs the ever-flowing dark blood of his don's deeds. He is one among the litany of the lost who run rampant and raise ratings in their purchase of podiums.

Bob paces between bed and television set. There will be no more "button, button, bellybuttons," but rather a man so utterly focused on willing the world from ruination to reverie that he believes red-beaked birds are dressing him in the armor of Theseus. The talking head traitors to country and flag will fall to a symphony of infamy from that composer of Bob's own selection, validating his V formation of chirp-song valets and the varied voltages of victory. Time has come to remove parrots from perch.

—

IN AN OPPOSITE ORCHESTRATION to despair, Morricone's "Gabriel's Oboe" makes its cellular rise in Bob as night falls on the face of the Lincoln Monument. He boards bus and savors the float he feels in the feast of reflective window refractions. A counter-directional dance to what is actual of those refractions reconstituted. When he arrives at that manageable mile from his target-epicenter, he disembarks into a London fog, his lumbering form siphoning a trail through its mist. Forms of former factories peak through portions in shadow and smothering gloom. Bob finds his path to the foot of a transformer still functioning like a goliath as yet un-ghosted by David. He puts his ear to its steel, sensing the sweet spot, and with the slaying sensation of a boy barker breaking bargain with the social contract, he allows the lines to blur between melee and range weaponry, wielding his magnificently machined mallet overhead, its arching so masterful and merciless as it strobes against the night sky. On impact, its H-hour may be the pressing of play to amplification. Concentric circles of vibratory reaction here, no simple pebble in a lake. This one, its equal and positive reaction calculates origin to radius without consideration of clockwise momentum. By design, a broken digital watch, in its liberation from harmonic oscillation, picks twenty-four perfect hours, perspectus, and penetration through the jaded geometry of all previously programmed laws of science to produce a virulent strain of voltage and spherics, winding from his impact's energy whirlpool to White House.

The music makes the marble face of time smile before Bob. Now more than ever, his pragmatic spirituality will require not optimism but rather strict beholdence to the religion of existence as energy. The loop of magnetic fields, current flowing in aggressively opposing directions, trains on parallel tracks. Loops that are twisted close together produce the AC/DC fields of his fancy. He yearns to embody what Didion described as "what we once called character." In this value of permittivity, oboe, and strings, Bob secures the mallet over his shoulder and across his back as though returning an arrow to its quiver. He hears the vibratory forces rising and the origin of the reactive chain. Coruscation confirms ferocity of fuze. He sets a cellphone at his feet, submits a text, un-assing[23] the X. He sets his sights on a distant rooftop bar and best of topographical crest. Moving in its direction, first at slow trot, accelerating to canter, and finally a full and bounding gallop through the city streets saddled with the science of

---

23   Military slang for exit position.

Bob's mind as the emerging domino trail of transformer explosions, antenna transmissions provoked, magnetic fields flashing, the foraging of charges into a squeeze, rendering them crushed cans in capacitors. Sparkage spelling the search for smart grid access, sources, gains, and velocity. From entilade to oblique, his fire, a freak.

Bob's flight feeds him through the door of the W Hotel. He trades elevator for stairs, bounding skyward until, in a huff and puff, he finds himself entering into the tower's top floor to the Point of View Bar with its spectacular citywide view. From that vantage point, Washington, DC, a sea. Its wave of arcing lights on approach move like a million-head herd of rats in magnesium-glare scintillation. The dance of magnetically moving metals like the jet engine rippling a face of proximate skin. This is an electrical light ballet, mesmerizing as Morricone. As his mental music swells, Bob senses his own conceits drawn in witness to the wonder of his own work and in contrition turns and moves to the bar. Sitting himself on a stool, the display of his craft plays out reflected in a mirror only partially blocked by the colored bottles of anti-ecumenical liqueurs. Simultaneously, patrons move, drawn by the flickering lights flaring from the city below in the glass of floor-to-ceiling bar windows, highlighted by a thunderous soundwave of circuitry advancing ever closer. The patrons gather and tighten beside the panes, processing a palette from wonder to worry.

"What in the world could be going on down there?"

"Are we safe here?"

If only one could get a frightened crowd to lend an ear…and if one could, this is what they'd hear (to animists, it's clear): that Bob had birthed a baby, its Bethlehem to soon appear. It doesn't like to be called "Sparky," though that's likely the name it will wear. Neither boy nor beast not a girl in the least, but best you take it from the source, a voice of voltage and of force:

"I'm no different than you. Not anymore. We are all just circuits and slaves of fiber-optic cyber systems marching us into mayhem. You can't shut me off and you can't shut me up (like you tried to Arabs and others after 9/11, nor men after #MeToo). Pandora's box is open and I'm here to fuck it. So, behold as I slither serpentine, hop, skip, and jump. My target discrimination, an elaborate imitation. I manipulate the microwaves and calculate my course. My per-second propagation? Two hundred ninety-nine million seven hundred ninety-two thousand, four hundred fifty-eight meters in a vacuum. I can downshift on a dime to skips of charge over twelve-gauge copper wire-carries of ten-ampere DC current, making my electron drift velocity eighty centimeters per hour. So, as you can imagine, I'm on a bit of a roller coaster here. But fuck it, life is full of ups, downs, twists, and turns. I'm tweaking and torquing and spinning on my head, playing hopscotch in a feast of fire. I'm pissing violet rays and alternating currents on Tesla's grave. I'm not nostalgic. I'm now, baby. I'm THE now baby. The baby of Bob. Bob Honey. I'm the stuff he do. And I ain't the first being of inconsistent quantum. I hope I'm not asking you to take too much 'a leap! Get it? Quantum? Leap? I don't mean

to toot my own horn, but I am hot, man. The autoignition to detonate methane (dependably) is one thousand one hundred twelve if you're going on Fahrenheit, that's (F) for all you fuckers, and five hundred forty Celsius, that's (C) for all you cunts. Do I sound angry? YOU'RE DAMN TOOTIN' I'M ANGRY! I'm electric. Eccentric. Eclectic. And charged as Strawberry-Apple Pie White Lightning Moonshine. Six zillion proof. Remember, I told you a few sentences ago, I'm hot? I'm even hotter now. Overtaking spark plugs by laser ignition. Check it! Watch me dazzle, deflower, and dance. Oh! There's a conductor! Conduct this, bitch! I'm crushing substation control points. From subterranean to tower-top and all that's betwixt and between—initiating transformer collapse and pulling from peak-hour demand. Everything but me in blackout. I'm flying through your electrical infrastructure and you don't even know my name. An object in motion wants to stay in motion, not watch the witless cumming of humor's mediocrity and the figless Newton of an unformed face. Just when you think I'm going this way...ZING! I go the other. Whoops, what's that, a light post? Did I just short that thing? Did its line swing across the street? Start a fire in a field? Did the fire just start a spark in the substation next door? It did indeed. I did. And, baby, I'm a hell-bound tumult train. I've got your house of white in sight. My daddy reared me independent of grid. I dial sabotage into system of wireless smart meters and gas sensors to gain buildup in fuel. All that infrared spectroscopy ain't got nothing on me. And now I have come to the White House gate. Its sewer I have come to penetrate. My creeper

wires will elongate through the impenetrable mesh of its
Faraday crate. It's funny, you know, existence I mean. The
wilder you live, the more likely you end up in the shitter.
Let's call this E^{24} minus zero-six-niner and counting..."

—

IN BLACKOUT, THE BARMAN appears before Bob. He flicks
on a flashlight, illuminating his face from below (are faces
different when lit from below?[25]). A familiar smile. It is,
again, El Greco Hernandez. El Greco, who wears jockstrap
medals[26] on the outside of his pants.

"Are you serving?" asks Bob.

To which El Greco responds, "I am always serving."

"That clock..." Bob says, referring to one above the
bar, "...does it keep accurate time?"

"Perfect time. It's on an independent battery," responds
El Greco.

"Good."

"What can I do for you?"

Bob slides a piece of paper across the bar. "Could I ask
you to place a call to that number, please? Let it ring once,
then hang up."

—

BACK WHERE BOB LEFT it, the cell phone is set to autodial
the switchboard at 1600 Pennsylvania Avenue. It rings a

---

24   Countdown to encounter.

25   William Golding, *Lord of the Flies.*

26   Medals never to be seen, bestowed upon covert operators.

single ring, clicks into calling mode, and begins to sing. Nearby, a drifter listens to its song, a short little ditty, though its message is long. When the White House receives it, Bob's recorded voice is looping along.

Jim crack corn and I don't care,
Jim crack corn and I don't care,
Jim crack corn and I don't care,
the White House will
short-ly dis-ap-pear.

—

BACK AT THE POINT of View Bar, patrons overlook the action exclaiming exodus from White House grounds. "Oh my God, look. What are they doing?" asks one.

"It looks like an evacuation," answers another.

"Fucking A-rabs. They're at it again!" resolves another.

Meanwhile, as Bob sips from a piña colada, "Too much predisposition to the pejorative," comments El Greco.

Bob barely gets the words out, "Yes, it is disturbing..." when a building-shaker of a blinding white flicker-flash kicks off the shuttering bar mirror into Bob's eyes, its source sending patrons into scramble and scream. This illumination is immediately followed by a resounding BOOM!!! of resonant report. When the windows of the bar belly inward and shatter, a blast wave of extruded executive branch excrement and its methane's balm make bold entry. Patrons flee flying shit-splashed shards in horror. Bob barricades his olfactory entries with napkins soaked in the sweet coconut cream of his colada. As ever,

El Greco, unfazed in the fugazi, assumes to serve who next may long for libation.

With that, Bob pays out, countering and evading the vomits of the fleeing crowd.

As he steps up toward the view, comes El Greco's adieu. "Alpha-Mike-Foxtrot, hope you achieve your objective," he spews.

Bob's response: "Shway-shway."

Bob is standing on the high edge of the now window-less sill. Below, the White House and its grounds, a sinkhole to liquefaction being simultaneously supplanted by the rising black and bubbling crude of pooey presidential expenditures. Bob perceives the cell phone flash, turning to find he has been joined by a woman beside the sill. She wears stiletto heels, a Brazilian tan and thong. She, the self-declared third satellite of Bob's syzygy, queen of Instagram and suspected bomber of all things yellow. She, the symbol of social technology's most salacious self-indulgence. New technologies so significant in the saving of lives and perhaps a simple satisfaction of one's yearning to share daily details, if within an otherwise existing trust—these same technologies, so utterly useless and undignified in the conceit that they may be the creator of either. There she be, the embodiment of exhibitionism's self-deceit.

"Hello, Bob," rings the return of Anasyrma.

"Oh," says Bob. "You. The *poster*. The one people tell everything to."

"I'm so happy you remember me, Bob. I have more followers than ever. I mention you quite often."

"You mention me?"

"Yes, Bob. Do you know what Deepfake is?"

Bob shakes his head. Anasyrma begins to cackle. "Oh, I think you'd be quite amused, Bob. I can put anything I want in your mouth and make you say it."

"Really?"

"Oh, yes," answers Anasyrma. "I can and I do. You should follow me."

"I can't follow you," explains Bob. "I'm afraid of falling." With that, Bob shoves Anasyrma and her selfie stick from the sill. Throughout her fall, she captures her final moments, pressing a group *send* in the millisecond before her body's ultimate impact on pavement.

—

ABOVE, SILHOUETTED IN THE despoiled sill, Bob briefly lingers. Before him, an incision upon iconic structure by means of both unsentimental and surgical circuitry. All had gone perfectly according to plan. The seeming survival of humans from the utter decimation of a shamed address. Still, a nagging, dragging feeling begins to fill Bob head to foot. Could this area of operations be the albatross of a man now obsolete? And why, for the first time in Bob's memory, had he planned no further than the action itself? No safehouse or haven, no person or place planned or waiting for a man whose nature knows only to proceed at pace.

—

ON THE STREET OUTSIDE the hotel, Bob exits the building, stepping over the deconstructed form of Anasyrma, who—always attuned to fashion—has pooed her thong. And though reduced from body to deflated bag of bones oozing liquefied organs from every orifice, she fits right in with the shit, darkness, and frenzied fugazi of the scene outside. Bob's nostrils bulging with wetted white napkin as the unprotected and panicked public gasp, gurgle, and 'gurgitate, lungs marinating in the atomized stench of presidential dump. Their poor souls unprotected by the sweet essence of coconut crème, pineapple, and rum. Now, the approach of a low-flying insertion helicopter, its night sun strobing the shithole below in a conservative cathedral of light. It scans the scene like a prison tower beam, White House evacuees revealed, scattering in every direction. Rotor-wash casts a whirl of sewage splatter as the bird lowers over the blast zone.

Bob, undetected, takes cover, crouching conveniently behind the car valet's clear plastic podium. He spies boots hitting the helo's skids; they push off and fast ropes deploy as armed men in hazmat suits descend into the muck. First among them, bullhorn carabinered to his hip, a solider of imposing stature, the same raid commander Bob had spied through his gun yard peephole. He whose face appeared a patchwork of harvested human tissue. He who brings bullhorn to lips, announcing his authority over the action. On Sixteenth Street, a convoy of Secret Service vehicles— the leading one with a winch is hauling what looks like the porcine president from the swamp by cable. There can be no fanfaronade in his fashion of flurry-go-nimble.[27] Once pulled onto the deck, a medic plunges his chubby chest. Identification confirmed while dislodging squitters he'd swallowed in the blast. His detail, disgusted, begins to flee like the flying monkeys of Oz as a Slovenian pulls herself out from the soup by chain migration. Bob knows when it's time to get off the X. Though not registered as a foreign object, he stands from his crouch, lifting the valet stand with the top of his head, letting it wrap him like a riot shield against a world of whirling shit.

---

27   Old Cornish word for diarrhea.

INTERLUDE

TRANSCRIPT

SHERIFF'S BLOTTER—WOODVIEW COUNTY, CALIFORNIA
WEDNESDAY, MARCH 15

"911…WHAT'S YOUR EMERGENCY?"

"He's got kike-nigger blood. A faggot-tranny who bleaches his fat skin like that skinny Jackson pedophile…"

"I'm sorry, sir. Do you have an emergency to report? Can you tell me your name, please?"

"I'm tellin' you, I know this bitch. And he is a bitch. A fuckin' half-cunt feminist fairy fucker!"

"Sir, I'm going to have to ask you to tell me your name."

"My name? My name is American. My name is not some Mexican jumpin' bean, stealin' jobs, slingin' dope, or fuckin' your wife…"

"Sir, your name and your emergency, PLEASE."

"My name is Harry Helen Mayo—"

"Middle name Helen?"

"That's right—Helen. Son of a white woman name'a Helen Mayo Jr. and grandson to my white-skinned wonderful granny, Helen Mayo Sr., may she rest in peace."

"I'm familiar with your family, sir. What's your emergency?"

"My emergency, dipshit, is your emergency too. What world you livin' in? It's him, I tell you. That fat fuck, tree-prunin' prick! He did it."

"Did what, sir?"

"He was forever makin' these silly signs. Silly-ass signs sayin' nothin' but sinister shit. My mother and grandmother both had his number. Oh, boy, did they. And I believe they paid with their lives. Yes, I do. In both their deaths, I suspect foul play, but that's a conversation for another day. Just when we had the chance for the great white way, this fuckin' fat weirdo liberal blows up our great leader's house, and may I remind you our house...the WHITE House! WHITE! WHITE! WHITE!"

"Sir, this is what I'm going to do. I'm going to go ahead and pass this information on to the FBI. I'm sure they'll contact you immediately and you can share this information with the agency. So, I'll just ask you to stay by your phone."

"Stay by my phone? I'm not talking to any fuckin' FBI agents. It's in your lap now. Don't say I didn't warn you."

"Warn me, sir?"

"Oh, you fuckin' idiot. You fuckers never listen to white people. Never listened to the Mayo family. Be it known we rang the bell. Now, I tell you what I'm goin' to do. I'm goin' to write Ms. Laura Ingraham a letter, 'cause we are meant for each other. And I will let her know of my unending devotion. Then I'm goin' to prove it and light an atheist's house on fire. Once I've done that, maybe you lazy limp dicks will get off your nigger-lovin' asses. Don't bother comin' after me, 'cause I'll be

making Laura kiss me deep in my mouth with my mother's magnum.
THREE-FIVE-SEVEN, MUTHAFUCKAS!"

[Click.]

The caller disconnects.

STATION FIFTEEN

DAMNED BY FEIGNED PRAISE

A ND WHAT OF THE Buddhas of Bamiyan in the valley
of Hazarajat? These two sixth-century sites under
UNESCO stewardship until dynamited by Mullah Omar
in a Taliban declaration of opposition to idols or protest
to famine. While Bob was no connoisseur of sandstone
carvings, nor a worshipper of gods he'd never known, he
could still recall the wince he'd felt at the reporting of this
loss to the curiosities of human history. Similarly, when
Congress castrated the face of a cocksucker testifying to
committee, the memory of his once brutish, bullying,
and leveraging of law on behalf of his boss succumbed to
rebirth by beautiful humility.

Here he is in full view, the landlord's former lawyer.
That face once so full of fatuous arrogance is suddenly
softened by evidence undeniable, the lawyer's existential
ascendency exposed. In this man's face, so full of fear and
shame, Bob sees his own, and by extension, an empathy

engages. Even from depravity, a flicker of decency in a flame begging, clawing, surrendering for some slight trickle of a return to dignity. So it is that all men of purpose must at some point sink their feet into the piles of sand, mud, and straw, their clocks reset by radioactive isotopes. And it's in the isotopes from straw that science signals time. How old is the soul that surrenders to a new beginning? This man's face, now walking backward through caves, cliffs, and memory. One foot behind the other, reversing beside fifth-century wall paintings, Sanskrit, and petroglyphs, a parading in vermilion robes, of the pride his children once had in him as he relives the glory days of their innocence to his isolation. In his most heathen state had he been thought a family's hero, and now, kneeling in apostasy... comes honesty. What would be Bob's? His mallet had turned to mud. His bombs filled his ears with sand, and his muscles are now made from straw. Branding can never again threaten his being. He is a man redeemable merely by the mercy of a grace as yet unimagined. And what of the ozone he'd given so much to defend? POP! POP! POP! Down go those decaying figures of foment to flatulence. Fuck guilt, fuck horror—but fuck them in a friendly way and call it a job well done. First and foremost must a man do his job well. Do stuff well, while others sell sell sell.

—

BOB RARELY RECOGNIZES THE ruses made up in his mind for endogenous rescue, but the truths…he saw them clean and clearly.

This is them:

He was good at engineering and sanitation.

He put on a mad fireworks display.

He was one hell of a pilot, sold a mean merkin, and most of all, had so well wielded a malevolent mallet, now reduced to mud.

He wonders if from that mud might one day come, of spontaneous generation,[28] a living thing, its origin a mallet. Since Aristotle and the ancient Greeks has man's solid science held a belief that beings began from nonliving decay. Perhaps one day his mallet might become a man. What matter might we have migrated from to become the people of our place today? The seeming civil of such seething incivility? There are devils in our DNA, while others may be made from tree bark or contaminated clay, fallen flowers or spores that dried, flaked, and fell to ground. Some might even be made from sound, selling so much speculative noise until we are pile driven by the constant pounding of corporate consciousness and the rubbernecking appeal of commercial magazines in a dentist's chair.

Yet what of one like Annie? Annie, whom he'd left in the mist of that Montenegrin monastery more than a year before, its cold cells and sisters a saddening sacrifice for her protection. He sees them circling her and chirping like the dingo dogs of a self-satisfied secret society's social clique. They take their vows to vouch for the unreal, like dear-dear friends. Yet Annie could not have come from

---

28   The production of living organisms from nonliving matter.

mud nor slime. She came from a park bench where the elderly bowled on lawns, sprung up as a flower from the grass. That ass. Those eyes. Bob cries…

Did a dingo steal my baby?

I don't know,
Do you?
I don't.
Feet
Breath
Beat
Piss
Poo
Perspiration
Dry mouth
Bubbling bile
The hallucination of being human
Hungerlessness
Motion
In movement…
Toward Maryland.
"Maryland? Why Maryland?"
I told you.
I don't know.

STATION SIXTEEN

RETURN OF THE POST-SLOVENIAN PRIESTESS

B ELOW THE MAIN HIGHWAY leading in and out of the capital, a shattered valet stand has been cast off, its scattered and sullied pieces parceled in the depth of a concrete culvert and slightly shivering in reverberation from the traffic above. Footprints peel from road to wetted field, and in the wood outside Washington: Bob.

Less striding than falling forward, he labors one slow step at a time, lamely leaving surplus for SoleMate.[29] Branches, brambles, then bridge, road, a passing bait truck, until a tiny town, a backyard carousel of painted ponies, its rusted bearings creaking with the turning of childhood's ghost. There were fences to climb, barbed wire and tire piles to mount and peer from, puddles surprising underfoot, and an American man who'd been so sure that what he'd done he'd had to do. And now: dread, doubt, an onslaught of didactic. Every organ

---

29   Law enforcement program used to identify shoe impressions.

feeling bloodied, benumbed, and enflamed. His deed, beginning to dog him, as if the putting down of a once beloved pet.

—

AFTER EIGHTEEN HOURS HOOFING it along railroad tracks and through boneyards, back roads, and alleys, Bob could finally breathe in Baltimore. Yet, standing in the North Charles thoroughfare, he becomes increasingly aware of building brackets of baseball fans on hajj to the holy land. Here now, Bob would have to un-as from public exposure before the crowds commune at Camden Yards.

The patina of a mansard roof, the brick veneer, and the limestone trim conspire to draw Bob's eye to the revolving doors of the Lord Baltimore Hotel across the intersection from where he stands. He crosses with some confusion as the big voice[30] of the stadium blurts the National Anthem with Fort McHenry[31] not far away.

"Has the game begun? What time is it? What season?" Bob realizes that his questions are not a function of confusion, but rather a reckoning that he has become part of the bigger American picture. The kaleidoscopic destiny of distraction where without questioning everything its viewer would fall for anything. Here where the big voice is booming through Baltimore, "Whose anthem is it anyway?" If not a symbol celebrating our right to stand, sit, or

---

30   Military slang for bullhorn or speaker system.

31   Birthplace of the National Anthem.

kneel…then instead perhaps a propaganda piece holding us hostage to a history written by long-dead victors.

Bob enters the hotel by a revolution of its door. He scans the foyer until his eyes land on the elevator bank. A waiting elevator opens in welcome. Bob crosses to it and enters. As if at random, he presses the key of its highest floor. The doors close and the lift ensues. That, the breath that only Bob can hear, in this, the brief aloneness of the lift. On the twenty-second floor, the doors open. Bob exits to the corridor. He begins a slow-paced walk, perusing each door as he passes, finally settling on a suite. He stops to scam the room with a door knock and a wad of cash, convincing the young couple in occupation that it was the last cash and wish of an otherwise homeless old man to isolate and rest, if only for the day. They exit, taking the cash, accommodating the privacy of his request. A wave of supernatural relief comes over him. The simple quiet and sublime solitude of a tidy space. He drops his pack where he stands, then moves gingerly into the bathroom, sits himself on the toilet, and removes his shoes, socks, pants, and shirt. Stands and drops his drawers. Twists on the shower handle, then reaches his hand into its strongly surging stream. Its warmth and steam building, he steps in. He lathers head to toe in fancy shower gel. He gets it all over him, suds up in every crack and crevasse, even forces his foamy finger into his navel. Once thoroughly rinsed, he twists the hot water handle to the off position, letting the chilly charge awaken his brain and close his pores. He steps out, feeling his way through the heavily steamed-up bathroom where his hand finds a towel. He dries himself, then twists off the cold water. As he makes his steam-blinded way to the sink, his wrist bumps a glass full of water. Taking this as a convenience, Bob gulps the water down, feeling finally purified. Standing in front of the slowly reappearing mirror, he hears the ringing of a phone from the adjacent bedroom. He moves toward it. Now from the bedside table, he lifts the phone. "Hello?"

"Hey, dude," says a slightly familiar voice. "It's me, the guy you let the room from."

Pensively, Bob responds, "Uh huh…"

"So there's a glass of water on the bathroom sink…"

"Uh huh…"

"You don't want to drink that, dude. My girl and I were gonna trip right before you knocked, and I don't know, we just kind of forgot when you gave us the money for the room."

"Forgot what?"

"That we left that glass there. She'd just laced it with like—"

"Seven hits of liquid lysergic acid?"

"Whoa, dude. How did you know that?"

"It's what happens when I let down my guard around glasses of water."

"That's weird. But, okay. I mean, we're cool. We don't need it back or anything. I just want to warn you before you gulped it down, but I guess I'm too late. You might want to consider making yourself vomit. That's a lot of hits. Okay, dude, that's our indemnification agreement. I'm off."

Bob stands listening to a phone gone silent. He catches himself in a crooked smile, a little speedy but not yet aware of any hallucinatory effect.

He moves back into the bathroom, where the steam has cleared and the mirror is clean. Yet, whoops, missing in the mirror is a reflection of Bob's mug. In place of face, jailhouse jackals and randy reapers outline the edges of his skeletonized skull.

From the hallway, the sounds of elevator doors opening and closing in thunderously slow echo. He re-enters the room, where its red velvet walls swim as lava lamps. Escalating demons dance among the visibly present intercellular and molecular particles. His ex-wife exits the television set in black and white and makes a run for the exit. Bob chases her, grabs her by her desaturated red hair, and swings her head around, exposing her face of leper-wolf now barking at him, the bark of a buzzing bee. He stands there completely still as the barking leper-wolf collapses at his feet in ash. Much of his room is now aflame. Its heat melts his hands like wax and the hands then vomit a wave of saltwater through the room, creating waves that break against the floral curtains, their flowers pulsing first toward Bob then receding. Extending then receding, he watches his melting hands.

Open. Close. Open. Close. Open.

Flowers become fists, their thick knuckles tense and flat. Their second joints move at the slow pace of deep-sea mollusks in an osculum inferno. Now, palms down, the veins bulge and pulse through common skin and the cut of surgeon's hands. He traces his fingers across his body and his fingers slice his flesh with scalpel-like ease. The voice of his ex-wife returns: "I HOPE YOU FUCKING DIE." Blood flow becomes a seeping gas fire and midget laughter hides in air ducts. The flash of a top-hat-wearing pig when one of the flowers from the curtain reforms into the ass of a large Negress. It leaps at Bob, swallowing him whole with the final closing slap of its sphincter.

From within this blackness comes a burning white light and the whisper, as if from a choir of birds, "In our room full of mirrors, I raped you. You raped me for the pain buried, and your weakness, my weakness…I feel you watch me…laughing." From where Bob stands, he gets a glimpse of the bathroom's marble floor. It begins to dance while bugs playing bugles march through the grouting between each marble square. Bob picks hairballs of undetermined origin from his mouth as the bugle-blowing bugs crawl up his body and into his eyes. He moves to sit at the edge of the bed, wondering if sleep may leave him dead, or worse, more deeply defined by disappointment.

—

SOME THIRTY-FIVE HOURS PASSED before Bob could break free from the kaleidoscopic colors of this nearly catastrophic chemical conflict. Now, sitting straight up and naked on the edge of the hotel bed, he sleeps. An incessant buzzing sound is building, bullying Bob back to consciousness. As his eyes slowly open, he registers the television before him. On it, an image of the aftermath of his deed. Blurring the camera's lens are billions of blue tail flies, swarming the former grounds of the White House. A reporter's voice draws the camera's attention to an anomaly of focus within the image's blur, like a portal in a cloud: a sign post made from the long handle of Bob's mallet and topped with a plate of plastic valet podium, there erected behind the rippled gates at the edge of the submerged White House grounds. Scrawled in feces on its facade, a slogan: "Buy a Honey of a property!" Bob raises the television remote, lowering the volume of buzzing flies and reportage. Now in silence, he again closes his eyes. He begins to track his own breathing.

"Button, button, bellybutton…"

> *Through the open suite window*
> *of a suite he'd commandeered*
> *his eyes Immune*
> *take flight*
> *toward the fears*
> *he'd never feared—*
> *Below*
> *the bloodied streets of Baltimore*
> *and buildings multitiered*
> *why do the dogs all seem to scatter*
> *as a marching sound grows near?—*
> *Rivers overflowing*
> *not with flies, but human rise*
> *for freedom's newborn heart*
> *the mandate of marchers' cries—*
> *BUY A HONEY OF A PROPERTY!*

There's your branding
As I said, I often lie
Not for fast food, fashion, or fascists
but for freedom's fateful cry.
Our house had been so soiled
before my circuit said, "Goodbye."
So dial 1-800-SUCK-IT!
I called the party line.
Now new, I see a city
sanitized by the sewage of that guy
on ascent to something clean
it appears before my eyes—
And the despotic darlings of our day
Invite an army of black flies
banking back over Washington,
a thermal lift to thinner air
then return to hotel hospice
and the solitude that one must dare.
Now I'll close the window,
sit in a silence oh so fair.
My tubby body breathing
what would kill a legionnaire,
My tubby body breathing
Over butt and penis bare...

There is a gentle knock on the door. Too tired for tactics, trepidation, or modesty, he rises naked and moves to the door, opening it unhesitant. There before him, the miracle of Annie, a bloody blade in hand, dripping drops of death into the hallway carpet by her feet. Noting the knife, Bob asks, "Is that yours?" With a slight shake of her head, she indicates in the negative, then nods down the hall. Bob leans forward to track her nod, where just feet away a big and bloodied ninja lies dormant.

"His name is Spurley Cultier Jr.," she tells Bob. "He was here to hurt you."

Their eyes engage. Dropping the knife, she studies his face, touches the skin, feels his exhaustion in her fingers. "You escaped the dingoes?" Bob asks.

"What dingoes?"

"Oh. I don't know. For some reason I thought you might be surrounded by dingoes. How are you here?"

She enters past him, her soft hand gliding a caress upon his face in passing. Bob allows the door to close behind him and turns to find Annie pulling something from a hidden part of his pack. It's the Polaroid of the two of them beachside in Venezuela. She bites the corner of the picture, making a tiny tear, and from inside the tiny tear, a tiny microdot.[32] She puts it in his hand for study. "I could never really lose you, my Bob-beam. You and I, ever a natural match in the division of labor."

He smiles gently, his eyes welling.

"Have you been watching television?" she asks.

"I had it on," he answers, "but fell asleep."

"So you don't know what's happening?"

"I know there's a mess in Washington and that flies are swarming the swamp. I know my eyes went wandering, but not if that's a real thing…"

---

32   Miniaturized tracking device.

"That's what you know?"

"Yes. I think I also know that you're here, but I'm not sure. I'm not sure that I'm here either." Annie sits him on the bed, putting herself beside him. Bob continues, "I know that energy exists, but that mine is lost. Is this Baltimore?"

"Sit-rep: It's not only Baltimore, my beautiful Bob-beam, but quite appropriately it is the Lord Baltimore Hotel, and quite specifically the presidential suite, one with a history of United States presidents occupying it. The youth rose up when the White House went down. They are a revolution looking for leadership. They've named him. Guess who?"

After a beat, Bob stumbles into a question. "Me? I'm guessing me."

"That's right, Bob. It's you."

Bob nods, offering Annie a sense of his skepticism and reemerging dread with the squint of his right eye, as if gravity were the gavel upon the guilty. That ever-increasing weight from the wake of any direct action's unintended consequences. Those too casually unconsidered then laid bare at a perpetrator's feet.

"Don't be a sore winner! It's the most incredible thing, Bob. The most incredible thing. The priest had called me to the rectory. When I arrived, his television was on, playing and replaying images of the White House swallowed from below. At first, I didn't understand what I was seeing, but I knew the world was watching it with me, wanting it with me. Our president's palace perishing into poo, and that's when it hit me…it must be you. I confessed there

BOB HONEY SINGS JIMMY CRACK CORN

and then to Father Dickie—his name's Ricardo, but we've grown close. I told him about you, and I know you won't like this, but we did something very naughty—we went online. A man named Mayo had figured from the sign on the lawn that it was you. He started posting accusations. Immediately, these posts were picked up. Tweets, retweets, Facebook friend to Facebook friend, but instead of being vilified, you were honored, Bob."

"I was honored?" Bob asks. "Honored for what?"

"For being mysterious in a world without mystery," she tells him. "A genius who couldn't take it anymore. A human for being human. You are being touted our *expert of efficacy*, and people are no longer numb. They're not, Bob, and because of you, they know it." There is an energy and passion in Annie's voice that Bob has only ever witnessed from women addressing others than himself. He feels its force as hot blood swells his groin. "They're not impressed anymore by the professionals of politics or business who meanwhile are so fucking amateur at life. Amateurs at love. 'Bob Honey does the stuff!' That's what they're saying, Bob. And a Honey of a president is what they want. All over the country, thousands of young people marching! The streets are alive. It took the White House vanishing for us to remember that we ourselves are here. MIT has already touted your mission a technological miracle. The Pope forgave himself for finding it all funny, and in West Covina, California, they're calling for you to be their city planner. New York City wants you as sheriff, and they don't even have a sheriff's department. Princeton

has appointed a panel of professors to update history books
with a chapter on you, Bob…but that's all small potatoes.
President, Bob. You're going to be president. President.
Of the new United States!" Hyperventilating, Annie takes
a pull from Bob's breath to catch her own.

He allows her to steady. To calm. To breathe until
her breath comes easily. "I would have to win an election.
Would I win an election?"

"Yes, my Bob-beam. As long as the manic exuberance
of socialists sustains, and…that you don't campaign."

"Okay," Bob says, his eyes devouring the fortitude of
her face, where its sight is registered like taste on tongue,
savored and sanctified by retinal absorption. This taste,
a menu item measuring his mortality. Little is lethal,
he thinks, that is not in a man's hand nor a woman's eyes.
She IS the high explosive to his low. She IS his girl. He
always thought so but could never know. And now, wow.

Annie looks to Bob shyly. "If you marry me," she
whispers, "that would make me First Lady. Will you marry
me, Bob?"

"Why do you want to be First Lady?"

Annie smiles. "I'm glad you asked that. Some would say
it's a step down. I left the nunnery as I was about to be can-
onized. So my other option was sainthood. I performed a
miracle…blah blah, which is to say, I do have my own things
going on. But—and tell no one this—Jesus's cock is long out
of service, so I vote no on nun. And anyway, men in robes
don't exactly melt my cookie. More importantly, love IS the
greatest miracle, Bob. And I want to make it with you."

"Okay," Bob says, "but I'm naked."

"Yes, Bob, you are. You can always be."

"And I have a little…" Bob says apologetically.

"Not so little now," says Annie, as her glance lifts from his crotch to his countenance. "Unbranded, unbridled, and free…with me," she affirms.

"Really?"

"Yes, really."

"Okay. Good. Because sometimes I just like to let my dick stick out."

"I know, Bob. I know."

"Because it feels good."

"I know it does, Bob. My beautiful Bob-beam. But we'll also get you a nice new suit, my president who can grab my pussy."

Fillylooing, Bob barks a towering tide of Tourette. "COME ONE, COME ALL, COME SLAY THE DRAGON!!!" He grabs the back of her well-glued wig, whirling her downward onto a presidentially endowed duvet between four pine posters of pathological paradise. Upon Bob's entry, Annie's virtuoso vibrations of von Bingen ring every bell in Baltimore until…

the wedding singer sings:

> *When I was young I us'd to wait*
> *on Massa and hand him de plate;*
> *Pass down de bottle when he git dry,*
> *And bresh away de blue tail fly…*

Jim crack corn and I don't care,
Jim crack corn and I don't care,
Jim crack corn and I don't care,
Ole Massa gone away.

EPILOGUE

Inching up toward inauguration, Bob maintained marriage while managing to leave the altar of leadership in Annie's youthful hands. The country had come to need nothing short of a miracle, he thought, one of recalibration and construction. Annie's résumé of near canonization qualified her for a swearing-in by a congress of grassroots constituents. Bob's objections to the objectionable had become, in his mind and heart, obsolete to optimism. His calculation went thusly: There is still a tiny twinkle in French eyes above the Hudson. A low-pitched pulse beneath a blindfold on Potomac. In '76, Paddy Chayefsky pulled no punches. And *hoary* was a word all its own. In 1977, Tony Kiritsis took his last stand In 1983, Tony Montana told the truth, even when he lied. Then said, "Say goodnight to the bad guy." In 1966, Leonard Alfred Schneider would die but not before declaring that the liberals can understand everything but people who don't understand them, and that Miami Beach is where neon goes to die, and that if you take away the right to say *fuck* you take away the right to say *fuck the government*. The government may yet give special counsel and intuition of institutions may still send signals similar to sanity. People, however, will remain the problem the cog in common humanity, climate, and conflict resolution. People are the problem and the things that can't be said anymore make life a bore. Sycophants of social media suck the conventional cock of censors' sensibilities volunteering complicity in common thought—they're bought! They're bullies, cunts, and cowards. Most too rich and showered, and in the ease of zeitgeist harmonization fatuous bully morons put sophomoric Twitter takedowns top on the list of "things (they) like to do." So convinced they're right, they yell it with all their might. Gesundheit! This sneezed-out phlegm of stewardship, now we sniffle as we pray the fear we'll fail the Earth has a price to pay. As cowards throw in the towel fleeing the sun's hot ray space travel boys claim mankind must move away. "Earth is not our last frontier..." This, we've heard them say. And they being men of gravity we let them put our fears at bay. But they can't see it coming, the reckoning of our rocket as it pulls away. That it's our mother we just left behind Ya feelin' proud today?

—

MEMORANDUM

FROM: The Office of the Deputy Director of ████████
CLASSIFICATION: DECLASSIFIED (Minimal Redaction)
DISTRIBUTION DATE: ████████

This memo is not for distribution and is intended for use by members of the ████████ and designated ████████ USG officials only.

SUBJECT: Project Rogue (STATUS: OBSOLETE)
MEANS OF RECOVERY: Triggered autonomous internal hotlist cyber monitors. Intercepted prior to distribution.

THREAT LEVEL: NEUTRAL

>   To: Mr. Robert Honey
>   RE: My Appetite for Rats
>   Sender: Mr. Spurley Osgood Cultier Jr.

Mr. Honey—

Yes, you've slipped me twice, but your time is near, and I'll be there. How in the heck did I ever suspect you would be subject to my blade in Baltimore? I mean of all places, BALTIMORE? How was it that I would be so prescient? Did you ever consider that within your own circle there might be a snitch? Did you have the hubris to believe you had no handler? I am going to so enjoy eating your stupidity, then crapping it out on your

old Woodview lawn. Yes, the very lawn Mrs. Mayo's
Chihuahua Nicky crapped on.

Sincerely,

Spurley Cultier Jr.

ANALYSIS and RECOMMENDATION:

As with previous memo dated ████████, current input
was written but unsent, and similarly without evidence
that Agent SPURLEY (formerly SHIRLEY) CULTIER JR.
AGENT ████–057 (**DECEASED**) was in possession of or
had knowledge of SUBJECT ROGUE whereabouts. It is the
finding of this assessment that Mr. Cultier's foreknowledge
of subject's movement to Baltimore may have been
influenced by a third party. Without speculation, this
analyst offers recusal and recommends further investigation
into any and all agents with knowledge of Project Rogue.

IN MEMORIAM by P. P.

They say it's always a woman who brings a man down, but not so for Bob, and neither was it Bob that got the best of me. That besting was the bulwark of a bald girl who most often goes blonde. A girl in whom Bob had found an absence of disturbance and a glistening between her legs. These could have been the clues this minister missed. I don't know if it's been the wine, the women, the sun, or cigarettes, but damn if I haven't grown older. I suspect Bob is now singing his own psalms somewhere under palms, but it's time that this man from Kentucky pass on his portfolio and return to the high hills, mountain leaves, and tappity-tap of the pileated pecker plundering pulp with pride in its plumage. When they can better a man like me, you know no lie is safe. And truth ain't worth the lyin' dreams of flying. You see, this is what happens when a novel's narrator sells out its own character.

Imagine if a nation did the same.

> Bob Honey prefers the tropics
> Bob Honey prefers the tropics
> Bob Honey prefers the tropics
> Bob Honey prefers the tropics
> Bob Honey prefers the tropics
> Bob Honey prefers the tropics
> Bob Honey prefers the tropics
> Bob Honey prefers the tropics
> Bob Honey prefers the tropics
> Bob Honey prefers the tropics

-THE END-

ACKNOWLEDGMENTS

THANKS TO PAUL THEROUX and Douglas Brinkley for their constant encouragement in the writing of this book. Also to Rare Bird, Tyson Cornell, and Guy Intoci, who knew how to thoroughly inspect the house without leaving me feeling the suspicions of Papa Bear, that "Somebody's been eating my words."

To Joseph Sacks and Sato Masuzawa for getting the devoted Luddite in me to succumb indirectly. To my son, Hopper, for ever riding the bomb, and my daughter, Dylan, for ever knowing the smile in its trajectory. To the love squad of Ma, Pa, and brother Chris, both here and gone.

To the critics of *Bob Honey Who Just Do Stuff*, the few who understood it, and the many who never read it. Without you, I may have shelved my typewriter for good. And finally, to those I've loved and lost in hostility, that they may recognize their characters in mine.